The Witch's Phantom

Fantasy fiction, Volume 13

Sarah Elizabeth Davis

Published by Arcane Horizons Publishing, 2024.

THE WITCH'S PHANTOM

First edition. August 9, 2024.

ISBN: 979-8224266937

Written by Sarah Elizabeth Davis.

Table of Contents

To those who embrace the magic within and dare to explore the shadows. This book is for the dreamers, the seekers, and the brave souls who believe in the power of love and redemption. May Seraphina and Thorne's journey inspire you to find courage in the face of darkness and hope in the most unexpected places.

In memory of my grandmother, whose enchanting stories and boundless love for the mystical world continue to inspire my writing.

Chapter 1: The Witch's Awakening

The sun dipped below the horizon, casting an amber glow over the dense forest that encircled the village of Eldergrove. Shadows lengthened, whispering ancient secrets that only the trees seemed to understand. At the heart of this mystical woodland stood an old, ivy-clad manor, its presence as formidable as the enchantress who had once inhabited it. The manor belonged to Seraphina Nightshade, a powerful witch who had recently inherited it following the mysterious death of her grandmother, Morgana Nightshade.

Seraphina stood at the edge of the forest, her eyes fixed on the imposing structure. She had returned to Eldergrove reluctantly, drawn back by duty and the unresolved questions surrounding her grandmother's demise. The villagers had always regarded Morgana with a mixture of reverence and fear, and whispers of her dark secrets had long permeated the air. Seraphina could feel the weight of those secrets pressing upon her as she approached the manor, clutching the key to a legacy she had yet to fully comprehend.

Inside the manor, the air was thick with the scent of herbs and old parchment. Dust motes danced in the fading light, casting an eerie luminescence over the centuries-old furnishings. Seraphina moved through the rooms with a mixture of nostalgia and unease. Every corner of the house held memories of her childhood, of lessons in magic and moments of quiet contemplation with her grandmother. But now, those memories were tainted by the inexplicable circumstances of Morgana's death.

In the heart of the manor lay Morgana's private study, a sanctuary of arcane knowledge and forbidden spells. The room was dominated by a massive oak desk, cluttered with scrolls, potions, and an assortment of mystical artifacts. At the center of the desk, atop a velvet-lined pedestal, rested Morgana's ancient grimoire. The grimoire was bound in dark leather, its cover embossed with intricate symbols that seemed to shift and writhe under Seraphina's gaze. She approached it with reverence, her fingers trembling as they brushed against its surface.

As Seraphina opened the grimoire, she felt a surge of energy pulse through her veins. The pages were filled with spells, incantations, and cryptic notes written in her grandmother's elegant hand. But it was the final entry that caught her attention—a hastily scrawled message that hinted at danger and a great secret.

"Beware the phantom's curse, for it seeks the bloodline's end. Only the chosen one can break it, but at great peril. Trust not the shadows, for they harbor deceit."

SERAPHINA'S HEART RACED as she read the words. Her grandmother had always been cryptic, but this message seemed urgent, desperate. She knew she had to uncover the truth behind Morgana's warning and the mysterious phantom it spoke of.

Driven by a mix of curiosity and duty, Seraphina spent the following days delving into the grimoire's secrets. She studied spells of protection, summoning, and banishment, determined to find a way to confront the phantom and the curse that threatened her bloodline. Her nights were filled with restless dreams, haunted by shadowy figures and whispered voices.

One stormy evening, as thunder rumbled in the distance, Seraphina prepared to perform a summoning spell she had discovered in the grimoire. The spell required a complex arrangement of runes, candles, and rare herbs. She meticulously followed the instructions, her hands steady despite the unease gnawing at her insides.

With the preparations complete, Seraphina stood at the center of the ritual circle, chanting the ancient incantation. The air around her crackled with energy, the candles flickering wildly as the storm outside intensified. As she reached the final words of the spell, a blinding flash of light erupted, and a gust of wind swept through the room, extinguishing the candles.

When the light subsided, Seraphina found herself staring at a figure materializing before her. The figure was tall and imposing, with eyes that glowed like embers and an aura of otherworldly power. This was Thorne, the phantom her grandmother's warning had spoken of.

Thorne's presence filled the room with an oppressive weight, and Seraphina could feel the raw energy emanating from him. He regarded her with a mixture of curiosity and contempt, his eyes narrowing as he took in her appearance.

"So, you are the one who dares summon me," Thorne's voice was deep and resonant, carrying a hint of menace.

Seraphina met his gaze, her fear tempered by determination. "I am Seraphina Nightshade, granddaughter of Morgana. I seek the truth behind my grandmother's death and the curse that binds you."

Thorne's expression softened slightly, a flicker of recognition in his eyes. "Morgana... she was a formidable witch. Her death was not of natural causes, that much I can assure you."

Seraphina's heart tightened at the confirmation of her suspicions. "Then tell me, what do you know of this curse and the danger it poses to my bloodline?"

Thorne hesitated, his gaze drifting to the grimoire on the desk. "The curse is ancient, born of a betrayal long forgotten. It seeks to eradicate your lineage, to sever the ties that bind you to the magical world. Only by breaking the curse can you hope to save yourself and your descendants."

"And how do I break it?" Seraphina demanded, her voice firm despite the fear gnawing at her insides.

Thorne's eyes met hers, a flicker of something akin to hope in their depths. "To break the curse, you must uncover the truth behind the betrayal and confront the one who cast it. But be warned, the path will be fraught with peril, and you may have to make great sacrifices."

Seraphina nodded, her resolve unwavering. "I am prepared to do whatever it takes to protect my bloodline and honor my grandmother's legacy."

Thorne regarded her for a moment longer before nodding. "Very well, Seraphina Nightshade. I will aid you in this quest, but know that my help comes at a price. I too seek freedom from the curse that binds me to this realm."

Together, Seraphina and Thorne began their journey into the unknown, bound by a shared goal and the secrets of the past. As they delved deeper into the mysteries of the grimoire and the curse that threatened them, they would uncover truths that would change their lives forever. The witch's awakening had only just begun.

Seraphina's journey into her grandmother's legacy was not without challenges. Each day brought new discoveries and dangers, testing her magical abilities and her willpower. The manor itself seemed alive with the energy of its former mistress, reacting to Seraphina's presence in ways that were both comforting and unsettling. She often felt Morgana's spirit watching over her, guiding her hands as she performed spells and crafted potions.

One evening, while poring over the grimoire, Seraphina discovered a hidden compartment within the desk. Inside, she found a collection of letters and journals, detailing Morgana's research into the phantom curse and the dark forces behind it. The writings revealed a tale of betrayal and vengeance, of a powerful sorcerer who had once been Morgana's ally but had turned against her in a quest for power.

As Seraphina read through the journals, she began to piece together the events that had led to her grandmother's death. The sorcerer, whose name was Alaric, had been consumed by jealousy and ambition. He had cast the curse upon Morgana's bloodline in a bid to eliminate her influence and claim her powers for himself. The phantom, Thorne, had been an unfortunate victim of Alaric's machinations, bound to the curse as both a guardian and a prisoner.

Determined to break the curse and bring justice to her grandmother's memory, Seraphina redoubled her efforts. She practiced her spells with newfound fervor, drawing strength from the knowledge that Morgana had faced similar trials in her own time. Thorne, ever watchful, offered guidance and insight, his own desire for freedom fueling his determination to help Seraphina succeed.

Their bond grew stronger with each passing day, an unspoken understanding forming between them. Seraphina found herself relying on Thorne's presence, his strength and wisdom a constant source of support. Yet, beneath the surface, she could sense the depth of his pain and the burden of his curse.

One fateful night, as the full moon cast its silver light over the manor, Seraphina decided to confront Thorne about his past. They sat together in the study, the flickering candlelight casting shadows on the walls.

"Thorne," Seraphina began, her voice gentle but firm, "I want to know more about you. About the life you led before the curse."

Thorne's eyes darkened, the memories of his past stirring within him. He took a deep breath, his gaze distant as he began to speak.

"I was once a sorcerer of great renown," he said, his voice tinged with sorrow. "I lived in a time of turmoil, where power was sought by any means necessary. I was ambitious, driven by a desire to master the arcane arts. But that ambition led me down a dark path."

He paused, the weight of his words hanging in the air. Seraphina listened intently, her heart aching for the pain he had endured.

"I became entangled with Alaric," Thorne continued, "a sorcerer whose thirst for power knew no bounds. We were allies, friends even, but his envy and greed twisted his soul. When he discovered my growing strength, he saw me as a threat. He betrayed me, binding my spirit to the curse in a bid to control me and eliminate Morgana."

Seraphina's eyes widened in shock. "So you were not just a victim of the curse, but also of Alaric's betrayal."

Thorne nodded, his expression grim. "Yes. My fate was sealed by his treachery. I have spent centuries bound to this realm, a phantom caught between life and death. My only hope of freedom lies in breaking the curse and exacting justice upon Alaric."

Seraphina's resolve hardened. She reached out, placing a hand on Thorne's arm. "We will break the curse, Thorne. Together, we will find a way to end this cycle of pain and restore balance."

Thorne met her gaze, a flicker of hope in his eyes. "Thank you, Seraphina. Your strength and determination give me hope that we can succeed."

As the night wore on, Seraphina and Thorne continued their study of the grimoire, searching for the key to breaking the curse. They knew the path ahead would be perilous, fraught with challenges and sacrifices. But they were ready to face whatever dangers lay in their way, united by a shared purpose and a bond that transcended time and space.

The witch's awakening had set into motion a chain of events that would alter the course of their destinies. As they delved deeper into the mysteries of the curse, they would uncover truths that would test their resolve and push them to the limits of their powers. The journey ahead was uncertain, but Seraphina and Thorne were determined to see it through to the end, no matter the cost.

Days turned into weeks as Seraphina and Thorne immersed themselves in the grimoire's secrets. They discovered that breaking the curse required not only magical prowess but also an understanding of the intricate web of relationships and events that had led to its creation. Morgana's journals provided invaluable insights, revealing the alliances and betrayals that had shaped the magical world of Eldergrove.

One particularly enlightening entry detailed a forgotten ritual known as the Rite of Severance. This powerful ceremony had the potential to break even the most formidable curses, but it required the caster to confront the source of the curse directly. The rite demanded immense magical strength and the willingness to sacrifice something of great personal value.

Seraphina knew that the Rite of Severance was their best hope, but the risks were daunting. She would need to gather rare ingredients, perform complex incantations, and face Alaric himself. The thought of confronting the sorcerer who had caused so much pain filled her with both fear and determination.

With Thorne's guidance, Seraphina began preparing for the ritual. They journeyed to distant lands, seeking out the rare herbs and mystical artifacts required for the ceremony. Each step of their journey brought new challenges and revelations, deepening their bond and testing their resolve.

One evening, as they camped by a serene lake, Thorne shared more about his life before the curse. He spoke of his family, his dreams, and the moments of joy and sorrow that had defined his existence. Seraphina listened intently, her heart aching for the man who had lost so much.

"I had a sister," Thorne said softly, his gaze fixed on the shimmering water. "She was my anchor, my confidante. Losing her was the hardest part of all this."

Seraphina reached out, taking his hand in hers. "I'm sorry, Thorne. I can't imagine the pain you've endured."

Thorne squeezed her hand gently. "Thank you, Seraphina. Your compassion means more to me than you know."

As they sat in silence, a shooting star streaked across the sky, a symbol of hope and renewal. Seraphina felt a renewed sense of purpose, determined to see their quest through to the end.

Upon returning to Eldergrove, Seraphina and Thorne set to work preparing for the Rite of Severance. They gathered the ingredients, inscribed the runes, and rehearsed the incantations. The night of the full moon approached, the chosen time for the ritual.

On the appointed night, the manor was filled with an aura of anticipation and dread. Seraphina stood at the center of the ritual circle, her heart pounding with a mixture of fear and determination. Thorne stood beside her, his presence a comforting anchor.

As she began the incantation, the air around them crackled with energy. The candles flickered, casting eerie shadows on the walls. Seraphina's voice grew stronger with each word, the power of the ritual building to a crescendo.

At the final word, a blinding light enveloped the room, and a figure materialized before them. Alaric, the sorcerer who had cast the curse, stood before them, his eyes burning with malice.

"So, the witch and the phantom seek to defy me," Alaric sneered. "You will find that the power of the curse is beyond your comprehension."

Seraphina met his gaze, her fear replaced by a steely resolve. "We will break the curse, Alaric. Your reign of terror ends tonight."

A battle ensued, the clash of magical energies filling the room with blinding light and deafening sound. Seraphina and Thorne fought with all their might, their bond and determination driving them forward. Alaric's power was formidable, but Seraphina's magic, fueled by her love for her family and her desire for justice, proved to be a match for him.

In a final, desperate act, Seraphina invoked the full power of the Rite of Severance. The room was engulfed in a blinding light, and a powerful surge of energy coursed through her. She felt a part of herself being torn away, the sacrifice demanded by the ritual.

When the light subsided, Alaric lay defeated, his power shattered. The curse that had bound Thorne and threatened Seraphina's bloodline was broken. Thorne, now free from his phantom form, stood before her as a mortal man.

Seraphina collapsed to the floor, exhausted but triumphant. Thorne rushed to her side, his eyes filled with gratitude and love.

"You did it, Seraphina," he whispered, his voice choked with emotion. "You broke the curse."

Seraphina smiled weakly, her strength waning. "We did it, Thorne. Together."

As dawn broke over Eldergrove, the manor was filled with a sense of peace and renewal. Seraphina and Thorne, their bond stronger than ever, looked forward to a future free from the shadows of the past. The witch's awakening had brought not only the end of a curse but also the beginning of a new chapter in their lives, one filled with hope, love, and endless possibilities.

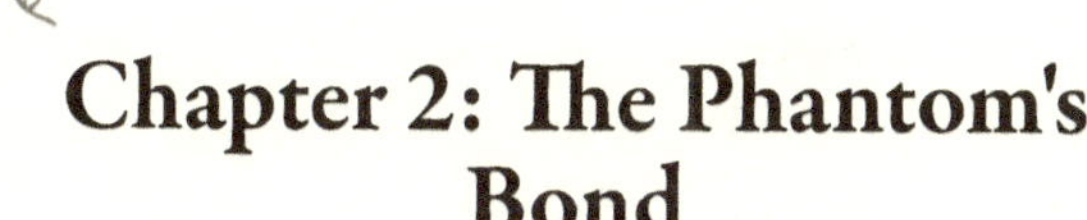

Chapter 2: The Phantom's Bond

The dawn's early light filtered through the ancient, stained-glass windows of the Nightshade manor, casting colorful reflections on the stone floors. Seraphina sat at the heavy oak table in the study, the grimoire open before her, its pages filled with arcane symbols and cryptic notes. The events of the previous night lingered in her mind—the battle with Alaric, the breaking of the curse, and the transformation of Thorne from phantom to mortal man.

Thorne stood by the window, staring out at the misty forest that surrounded the manor. The early morning light played on his features, highlighting the chiseled lines of his face and the intensity of his eyes. He seemed lost in thought, a man grappling with the enormity of his newfound freedom.

Seraphina watched him for a moment before breaking the silence. "Thorne," she called softly, her voice tinged with both curiosity and concern. "I think it's time we talked about your past and the bond that links us."

Thorne turned to face her, his expression grave. "Yes, you're right. There is much you need to know, Seraphina."

He moved to the table and took a seat opposite her. The weight of his presence filled the room, a reminder of the power and mystery that surrounded him. Seraphina leaned forward, eager to hear his story.

Thorne began to speak, his voice steady but filled with emotion. "I was born many centuries ago in a land far from here. My family was of noble lineage, and from a young age, I was trained in the arcane arts. Magic flowed through my veins, and I quickly became one of the most powerful sorcerers of my time."

He paused, his gaze distant as if seeing the events of his past unfold before him. "But with great power came great ambition. I sought to master all forms of magic, to uncover secrets that had been lost to time. My quest for knowledge led me to dark places, to alliances with those who were not to be trusted."

Seraphina listened intently, her heart aching for the pain Thorne had endured. "Is that when you met Alaric?" she asked gently.

Thorne nodded. "Yes, Alaric was a fellow sorcerer, skilled and ambitious like myself. We became allies, bound by a common goal. But Alaric's ambition was tainted by envy and greed. He saw my growing power as a threat, and in his desperation to surpass me, he betrayed our alliance."

A shadow crossed Thorne's face as he continued. "He cast a powerful curse upon me, binding my spirit to the mortal world as a phantom. I became trapped between life and death, a guardian and a prisoner bound by a curse that could only be broken by confronting the source of the betrayal."

Seraphina's eyes widened with understanding. "And that source was Alaric."

"Yes," Thorne replied. "For centuries, I was bound to this realm, my spirit unable to find peace. It was a fate worse than death, a constant reminder of my failure and Alaric's treachery."

Seraphina reached across the table, placing her hand over Thorne's. "I'm so sorry, Thorne. I can't imagine the pain you must have endured."

Thorne met her gaze, his eyes filled with gratitude. "Your compassion means more to me than you know, Seraphina. But there is more you need to understand. The curse that bound me was not just a punishment for my actions. It was also tied to an ancient bond that links us."

Seraphina's brow furrowed in confusion. "An ancient bond? What do you mean?"

Thorne took a deep breath, his expression serious. "The Nightshade lineage and my own bloodline are connected by a powerful bond, one that was forged long before either of us was born. It is a bond that transcends time and space, a link that ties our fates together."

Seraphina's mind raced as she tried to comprehend the implications of Thorne's words. "But how? How are we connected?"

Thorne's voice was steady as he explained. "Many generations ago, our ancestors formed a pact, a union of magic and blood that created a bond between our families. This bond was meant to ensure that our combined powers would protect the magical world from great evils. But when Alaric betrayed me and cast the curse, it disrupted the balance of that bond. It became a curse that threatened both our bloodlines."

Seraphina felt a chill run down her spine. "So, breaking the curse was not just about freeing you. It was about restoring balance to our bond."

"Exactly," Thorne said. "And that is why our destinies are intertwined. You have the power to unlock the secrets of the grimoire, and I have the knowledge to guide you. Together, we can uncover the truths that have been hidden for centuries and restore the balance that was disrupted."

Seraphina nodded, her resolve strengthening. "Then we will work together, Thorne. We will unlock the secrets of the grimoire and uncover the truth behind the ancient bond. And we will do whatever it takes to protect our bloodlines and the magical world."

Thorne's eyes glowed with determination. "Thank you, Seraphina. Your strength and courage give me hope that we can succeed."

As the morning light continued to fill the room, Seraphina and Thorne turned their attention to the grimoire. They knew that their journey would be fraught with challenges and dangers, but they were ready to face them together. The bond that linked them was a source of strength and power, and they would need every bit of it to uncover the secrets of the past and forge a new future.

Over the following days, Seraphina and Thorne immersed themselves in the study of the grimoire. The ancient tome was filled with spells, incantations, and detailed notes that provided insight into the magical practices of their ancestors. Each page seemed to pulse with a life of its own, as if the very essence of the Nightshade lineage was contained within its bindings.

As they worked, Seraphina and Thorne discovered that the bond between their families was more intricate and powerful than they had initially realized. The grimoire revealed that the pact formed by their ancestors had been sealed with a ritual known as the Union of Souls. This ritual had bound their bloodlines together, creating a link that allowed them to share knowledge, power, and protection.

One evening, as they pored over a particularly dense passage in the grimoire, Thorne suddenly looked up, his expression one of revelation. "Seraphina, I think I've found something important."

Seraphina leaned closer, her curiosity piqued. "What is it?"

Thorne pointed to a section of the text. "This passage describes a ritual called the Rite of Reflection. It is said to allow those bound by the Union of

Souls to see into each other's pasts, to understand the events that shaped their lives and the bond that connects them."

Seraphina's eyes widened with interest. "That could provide us with valuable insight into the nature of our bond and the events that led to the curse."

"Exactly," Thorne replied. "It may also reveal hidden truths about our ancestors and the pact they formed. But the ritual is complex and requires both of us to perform it together."

Seraphina nodded, her resolve firm. "Then we will do it. If it can help us uncover the secrets we seek, it's worth the effort."

They spent the next few days gathering the necessary ingredients and preparing for the Rite of Reflection. The ritual required a mirror imbued with magical properties, rare herbs, and specific incantations that would open a window into their shared pasts.

On the night of the new moon, they were ready. The manor was filled with an air of anticipation as Seraphina and Thorne stood before the mirror, their hands clasped together. The room was dimly lit by candles, their flickering flames casting an eerie glow on the walls.

Seraphina took a deep breath, her voice steady as she began the incantation. "By the power of the Union of Souls, I call upon the spirits of our ancestors. Reveal to us the truths of the past, the events that bind our bloodlines, and the secrets that have been hidden."

Thorne joined her, his voice resonant with power. "By the bond that links us, show us the reflections of our souls. Let us see into each other's pasts and understand the forces that shape our destinies."

As they chanted, the mirror began to shimmer with a silver light. The surface rippled like water, and slowly, images started to form. Seraphina and Thorne watched in awe as scenes from their pasts played out before them.

They saw the faces of their ancestors, the formation of the pact, and the powerful magic that bound their families together. They witnessed moments of triumph and tragedy, of love and betrayal. They saw the events that led to Alaric's betrayal and the casting of the curse.

Seraphina felt a deep connection to the images before her, as if she were experiencing the emotions and memories of her ancestors firsthand. She saw the love and dedication that had gone into forming the Union of Souls, and the pain and sorrow that had followed Alaric's treachery.

Thorne's past was equally vivid, filled with moments of joy and sorrow. Seraphina saw his childhood, his training in the arcane arts, and the bond he had shared with his sister. She felt his pain and anger at Alaric's betrayal and the despair of being trapped as a phantom for centuries.

As the final images faded, Seraphina and Thorne were left standing before the mirror, their hands still clasped together. The connection between them felt stronger than ever, a palpable force that transcended time and space.

Thorne's voice was filled with awe as he spoke. "The bond between us is more powerful than I ever imagined. It is a testament to the strength and resilience of our ancestors."

Seraphina nodded, her heart filled with determination. "And it is a bond that we will honor and protect. Together, we will uncover the secrets of the grimoire and restore balance to our bloodlines."

Thorne's eyes glowed with gratitude and hope. "Thank you, Seraphina. Your strength and courage give me hope that we can succeed."

As the night wore on, Seraphina and Thorne continued their study of the grimoire, their bond deepening with each passing moment. They knew that their journey would be fraught with challenges and dangers, but they were ready to face them together. The bond that linked them was a source of strength and power, and they would need every bit of it to uncover the secrets of the past and forge a new future.

The following days were a blur of activity as Seraphina and Thorne delved deeper into the grimoire's secrets. They discovered that the bond between their bloodlines granted them unique abilities and insights, allowing them to access knowledge and power that would have been impossible to attain on their own.

One of the most significant revelations came in the form of an ancient prophecy. Hidden within the grimoire's pages was a passage that spoke of a time when the descendants of the Nightshade and Thorne bloodlines would come together to face a great evil. The prophecy foretold that their combined powers would be the key to restoring balance to the magical world and protecting it from destruction.

Seraphina felt a sense of destiny as she read the prophecy. "This is why we were brought together, Thorne. Our bond is the key to fulfilling this prophecy and protecting our world."

Thorne nodded, his expression serious. "But the prophecy also speaks of great challenges and sacrifices. We must be prepared for whatever lies ahead."

As they continued their study, they discovered that the grimoire contained detailed instructions for a series of rituals and spells that would unlock their full potential. These rituals were designed to strengthen their bond, enhance their magical abilities, and prepare them for the trials they would face.

The first of these rituals was the Rite of Empowerment, a ceremony that would grant them access to the combined power of their ancestors. The ritual required a blend of their blood, enchanted crystals, and a series of incantations that would channel the energy of the Union of Souls.

On the night of the full moon, Seraphina and Thorne prepared for the Rite of Empowerment. The manor was filled with an air of anticipation as they stood in the center of the ritual circle, their hands clasped together. The candles around them flickered with a magical light, casting an ethereal glow on the room.

Seraphina's voice was steady as she began the incantation. "By the power of the Union of Souls, we call upon the spirits of our ancestors. Grant us the strength and wisdom to fulfill our destiny and protect the magical world from harm."

Thorne joined her, his voice resonant with power. "By the bond that links us, we seek to unlock the full potential of our combined abilities. Let the energy of our ancestors flow through us, empowering us to face the challenges ahead."

As they chanted, the crystals in the center of the circle began to glow with a brilliant light. The energy of the ritual surged through their bodies, filling them with a sense of power and connection. They felt the presence of their ancestors, their strength and wisdom guiding them.

When the ritual was complete, Seraphina and Thorne stood in silence, their bond stronger than ever. The energy of the Union of Souls flowed through them, granting them access to knowledge and abilities that had been hidden for centuries.

Thorne's eyes glowed with determination. "We are ready, Seraphina. With the power of our ancestors, we can face whatever challenges lie ahead."

Seraphina nodded, her resolve firm. "Together, we will uncover the secrets of the grimoire and fulfill the prophecy. We will protect our bloodlines and the magical world from destruction."

As the days turned into weeks, Seraphina and Thorne continued their study of the grimoire, their bond deepening with each passing moment. They uncovered new spells and rituals, each one bringing them closer to unlocking the full potential of their combined abilities.

One particularly challenging spell required them to venture into the heart of the enchanted forest, to seek out a rare flower known as the Moon's Tear. This flower was said to possess powerful magical properties, and its essence was needed to complete a crucial incantation.

The journey to find the Moon's Tear was fraught with dangers. The forest was filled with magical creatures and treacherous terrain, testing their skills and determination. But with Thorne's guidance and Seraphina's magical abilities, they navigated the challenges and eventually found the flower blooming in a hidden glade.

As they returned to the manor, Seraphina felt a sense of accomplishment and gratitude. "We did it, Thorne. With the Moon's Tear, we can complete the incantation and unlock the next level of the grimoire's secrets."

Thorne's eyes shone with pride. "Your determination and skill are truly remarkable, Seraphina. Together, there is nothing we cannot achieve."

With the Moon's Tear in hand, they prepared the incantation, following the grimoire's instructions with meticulous care. The ritual required them to infuse the flower's essence into a potion that would grant them access to the hidden knowledge within the grimoire.

As they completed the incantation, a surge of energy enveloped them, and the grimoire's pages began to glow with a brilliant light. New passages and spells appeared, revealing the next steps in their journey.

Seraphina's heart raced with excitement. "The grimoire is revealing its secrets to us, Thorne. We are one step closer to fulfilling our destiny."

Thorne nodded, his expression filled with determination. "We must continue our study and prepare for the challenges ahead. The path will not be easy, but with our bond and the power of our ancestors, we can overcome any obstacle."

As the weeks turned into months, Seraphina and Thorne's bond grew stronger, their combined abilities reaching new heights. They faced numerous challenges and dangers, each one bringing them closer to unlocking the full potential of the grimoire's secrets.

One of the most significant revelations came in the form of an ancient artifact known as the Eye of Eternity. The grimoire revealed that this artifact held the key to accessing the deepest levels of magical knowledge and power. But obtaining the Eye of Eternity would require a perilous journey to a distant land, where they would face powerful guardians and ancient traps.

Determined to succeed, Seraphina and Thorne set out on their journey, their bond and determination guiding them. The challenges they faced tested their skills and resolve, but with each obstacle, their bond grew stronger, and their abilities more refined.

After weeks of travel and trials, they finally reached the temple that housed the Eye of Eternity. The temple was a marvel of ancient architecture, its walls adorned with intricate carvings and symbols. But it was also filled with powerful guardians, magical traps, and challenges that tested their every move.

With Thorne's knowledge and Seraphina's magical prowess, they navigated the temple's challenges and eventually reached the chamber that held the Eye of Eternity. The artifact was a dazzling gem, its surface shimmering with a light that seemed to hold the secrets of the universe.

As they reached out to take the Eye of Eternity, a powerful force enveloped them, and the artifact's energy surged through their bodies. The bond between them deepened, and they felt a profound connection to the magical world and their ancestors.

With the Eye of Eternity in hand, they returned to the manor, their hearts filled with a sense of accomplishment and purpose. The grimoire's pages revealed new secrets and spells, each one bringing them closer to fulfilling the prophecy and protecting their bloodlines.

Seraphina and Thorne stood in the study, their bond stronger than ever. They knew that their journey was far from over, but with the power of the grimoire and the Eye of Eternity, they were ready to face whatever challenges lay ahead.

As they looked toward the future, they knew that their bond was not just a source of strength and power but also a testament to the resilience and determination of their ancestors. Together, they would uncover the secrets of the past, fulfill the prophecy, and protect the magical world from destruction.

The bond between Seraphina and Thorne was a beacon of hope, a reminder that even in the face of darkness and betrayal, the power of love, determination, and unity could overcome any obstacle. As they continued their journey, they knew that they were not alone. The spirits of their ancestors guided them, their strength and wisdom a constant source of support.

With the grimoire in hand and the Eye of Eternity by their side, Seraphina and Thorne were ready to face whatever challenges lay ahead. Their bond was unbreakable, their determination unwavering, and their love for each other and their bloodlines a powerful force that would guide them through the darkest of times.

Together, they would uncover the secrets of the past, fulfill the prophecy, and protect the magical world from destruction. Their journey was just beginning, and they knew that as long as they had each other, there was nothing they could not achieve. The phantom's bond had brought them together, and it would carry them through whatever trials lay ahead.

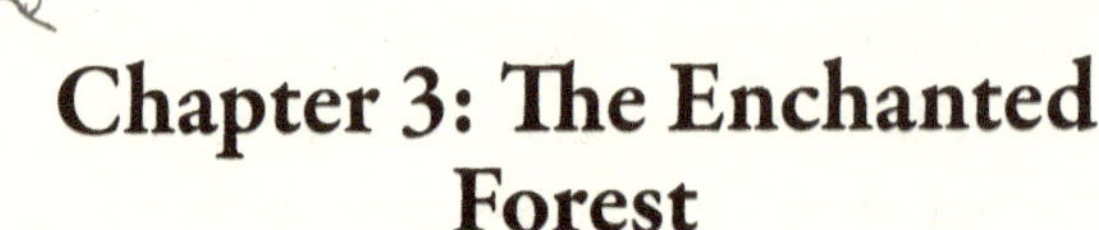

Chapter 3: The Enchanted Forest

The morning sun cast a golden glow over Eldergrove as Seraphina and Thorne prepared for their journey into the enchanted forest. The air was crisp, carrying the scent of pine and earth, and the manor seemed to hum with an anticipation that mirrored their own. Seraphina could feel the weight of the grimoire in her satchel, its secrets still only partially revealed. Today, they hoped to uncover more about the curse that had bound Thorne for centuries.

"Are you ready?" Thorne asked, his voice steady but his eyes reflecting a mixture of determination and apprehension.

Seraphina nodded, her resolve firm. "Yes. The forest holds many secrets, and I believe it will guide us to the answers we seek."

They set off, the path leading them into the heart of the forest. The trees loomed high above them, their ancient branches forming a canopy that filtered the sunlight into dappled patterns on the ground. The forest was alive with the sounds of nature—the chirping of birds, the rustling of leaves, and the distant call of a mysterious creature.

As they ventured deeper, the forest seemed to change. The air grew thicker with magic, and the trees took on an otherworldly quality, their bark shimmering with a faint, iridescent glow. Seraphina could feel the energy of the forest pulsing through her, amplifying her senses and heightening her awareness.

"We must be cautious," Thorne warned, his eyes scanning the surroundings. "The enchanted forest is known for its magical creatures, both benevolent and malevolent."

Seraphina nodded, her senses on high alert. They continued their journey, each step bringing them closer to the heart of the forest and, they hoped, closer to the answers they sought.

Their first encounter came in the form of a mischievous sprite, its tiny body flitting through the air like a hummingbird. The sprite's laughter echoed around them, a tinkling sound that seemed to come from all directions at once.

"Who dares enter the realm of the enchanted forest?" the sprite demanded, its voice high-pitched and playful.

"We seek answers," Seraphina replied, her voice calm and respectful. "We mean no harm."

The sprite hovered before them, its wings a blur of motion. "Answers, you say? The forest holds many secrets, but they are not given freely."

Seraphina glanced at Thorne, then back at the sprite. "We are willing to prove ourselves worthy. What must we do?"

The sprite's eyes gleamed with mischief. "A challenge, then. If you can solve my riddle, I will guide you further into the forest. Fail, and you must turn back."

Seraphina nodded. "We accept."

The sprite's laughter filled the air again. "Very well. Here is your riddle: I speak without a mouth and hear without ears. I have no body, but I come alive with wind. What am I?"

Seraphina pondered the riddle, her mind racing. She glanced at Thorne, who met her gaze with a look of encouragement. Suddenly, the answer came to her.

"An echo," she said confidently.

The sprite clapped its tiny hands in delight. "Correct! You are indeed worthy. Follow me, and I will guide you."

The sprite led them deeper into the forest, its flight path weaving through the trees with a grace that left Seraphina and Thorne struggling to keep up. As they moved, the forest grew denser, the magic more palpable.

Eventually, they reached a clearing, the ground carpeted with soft moss and dotted with luminous flowers. In the center of the clearing stood a majestic tree, its bark silver and its leaves shimmering with an otherworldly light.

"This is the Heart of the Forest," the sprite announced. "Here, you will find the answers you seek. But be warned, the forest tests those who come seeking its secrets."

Seraphina and Thorne approached the tree, its presence exuding a sense of ancient wisdom and power. As they touched the bark, a surge of energy coursed through them, and the forest seemed to come alive with a whispering chorus of voices.

"Welcome, seekers," the voices said in unison. "You have proven yourselves worthy to receive our guidance. What is it that you seek?"

Seraphina took a deep breath, her voice steady. "We seek the truth behind a curse that has bound Thorne to the mortal world for centuries. We seek to understand its origin and find a way to break it."

The voices murmured among themselves, the sound like the rustling of leaves in a gentle breeze. "The curse you speak of is ancient, born of betrayal and fueled by dark magic. To uncover its origin, you must delve into the past, to the time when the bond between your bloodlines was first forged."

Thorne stepped forward, his eyes filled with determination. "We are prepared to do whatever it takes to break the curse and restore balance."

The tree's leaves shimmered, and a vision began to form before them. They saw a time long past, when their ancestors had come together to form the Union of Souls. They witnessed the betrayal of Alaric and the casting of the curse that had bound Thorne.

But there was more. The vision revealed a hidden aspect of the curse—an artifact of great power that had been used to bind Thorne's spirit. This artifact, known as the Shadow Crystal, held the key to breaking the curse.

"The Shadow Crystal lies deep within the enchanted forest," the voices said. "It is guarded by powerful creatures and protected by ancient magic. To retrieve it, you must prove your worth and face the trials that await you."

Seraphina and Thorne exchanged determined glances. "We will do it," Seraphina said firmly. "We will retrieve the Shadow Crystal and break the curse."

The tree's leaves rustled, and the voices whispered their approval. "Very well, seekers. The path before you is perilous, but with your bond and determination, you can succeed. Go forth and may the magic of the forest guide you."

With renewed determination, Seraphina and Thorne set off deeper into the forest, their hearts filled with a sense of purpose. The forest seemed to respond to their resolve, the path before them illuminated by the soft glow of the magical flowers.

As they ventured further, the forest grew darker and more foreboding. The trees loomed high above them, their branches forming a dense canopy that blocked out the sunlight. The air was thick with tension, and Seraphina could feel the weight of the magic around them.

Suddenly, they heard a low growl, and a pair of glowing eyes appeared in the shadows ahead. A massive wolf-like creature emerged, its fur bristling and its fangs bared. The creature was clearly a guardian of the forest, and it did not look pleased to see them.

Seraphina and Thorne prepared for battle, their magical energies crackling in the air. The wolf-like creature lunged at them, its movements swift and powerful. Seraphina summoned a protective shield, deflecting the creature's attack, while Thorne unleashed a burst of energy that sent it sprawling.

But the creature was relentless, and it quickly recovered, its eyes burning with determination. Seraphina and Thorne fought with all their might, their bond and trust in each other guiding their movements. As the battle raged on, they began to understand the creature's tactics and adapted their strategy accordingly.

Finally, with a combined effort, they managed to overpower the guardian. The creature let out a mournful howl before disappearing into the shadows, leaving behind a glowing sigil on the ground.

Seraphina approached the sigil, her curiosity piqued. "What do you think it means?" she asked Thorne.

Thorne studied the sigil, his eyes narrowing in concentration. "It's a symbol of the forest's approval. We've passed the first trial, and the path to the Shadow Crystal is opening before us."

With renewed determination, they continued their journey, the sigil glowing brightly and guiding their way. The forest seemed to part before them, the path becoming clearer as they moved forward.

Their next challenge came in the form of a raging river, its waters churning with a powerful current. The river was wide and treacherous, and it seemed impossible to cross without being swept away.

Seraphina and Thorne stood at the riverbank, contemplating their next move. "We need to find a way across," Seraphina said, her mind racing for a solution.

Thorne nodded. "The river is infused with magic. We must use our abilities to find a way to navigate it."

They spent a few moments strategizing, and then Seraphina had an idea. "What if we use our combined magic to create a bridge of light? It would be strong enough to support us and allow us to cross safely."

Thorne's eyes lit up with approval. "Let's do it."

Together, they focused their energies, channeling their magic into a beam of light that extended across the river. The light solidified, forming a shimmering bridge that glowed with a radiant energy.

Carefully, they stepped onto the bridge, their hearts pounding with anticipation. The bridge held firm, and they made their way across the river, the current roaring beneath them. As they reached the other side, the bridge dissolved, leaving them standing on solid ground once more.

Seraphina let out a sigh of relief. "We did it."

Thorne smiled, his eyes filled with pride. "Our bond and determination are proving to be our greatest strengths."

With the river behind them, they continued their journey, the path becoming more treacherous with each step. The forest seemed to sense their presence, its magic growing stronger and more unpredictable.

AS THEY VENTURED DEEPER, they encountered a series of enchanted traps and puzzles designed to test their intelligence and teamwork. Each challenge required them to think creatively and rely on their bond to find solutions.

One particularly challenging puzzle involved a series of glowing stones arranged in a complex pattern. The stones emitted a magical energy that resonated with Seraphina's and Thorne's own energies, and they had to align the stones in the correct sequence to unlock the path forward.

Seraphina studied the stones, her mind racing to decipher the pattern. "I think each stone corresponds to a specific element of our bond. We need to match them to unlock the path."

Thorne nodded in agreement. "Let's try it."

They worked together, their combined knowledge and intuition guiding their actions. As they aligned the stones, the magical energy intensified, and the stones began to glow brighter.

Finally, with a final adjustment, the pattern clicked into place, and the path before them opened. The stones emitted a harmonious melody, a symbol of their success.

Seraphina and Thorne exchanged triumphant glances. "We're getting closer," Seraphina said, her voice filled with determination.

Thorne nodded. "The forest's challenges are testing our bond, but with each trial, we grow stronger."

With the path clear, they continued their journey, their hearts filled with a sense of purpose. The forest seemed to respond to their resolve, its magic guiding them ever closer to their destination.

As they approached the heart of the forest, they encountered the final guardian—a majestic stag with antlers that glowed with a radiant light. The stag stood tall and proud, its eyes filled with wisdom and power.

Seraphina and Thorne approached the stag with reverence, recognizing the significance of this final trial. The stag's presence exuded a sense of calm and strength, and they knew that they had to prove their worth to pass.

The stag spoke, its voice deep and resonant. "You have journeyed far and faced many challenges. To prove your worth, you must demonstrate the strength of your bond and your commitment to your quest."

Seraphina stepped forward, her voice steady. "We are ready. What must we do?"

The stag's eyes glowed with approval. "You must perform the Rite of Unity, a ceremony that will solidify your bond and unlock the full potential of your combined powers. Only then will you be worthy to retrieve the Shadow Crystal."

Seraphina and Thorne nodded, their resolve unwavering. The stag guided them to a sacred clearing, its ground covered with soft moss and surrounded by ancient trees.

The Rite of Unity required them to channel their energies into a single, unified force. They stood facing each other, their hands clasped together, their hearts and minds aligned.

As they began the incantation, the air around them shimmered with a brilliant light. The energy of their bond surged through them, intertwining their magic and strengthening their connection.

The stag watched with approval, its presence a calming force. "Focus on your bond and let it guide you."

Seraphina and Thorne continued the incantation, their voices harmonizing with the forest's magic. The energy around them intensified, forming a radiant aura that enveloped them.

When the Rite of Unity was complete, the clearing was filled with a sense of harmony and balance. Seraphina and Thorne felt a profound connection, their bond stronger than ever.

The stag bowed its head in approval. "You have proven your worth. The path to the Shadow Crystal is now open."

With the stag's blessing, they continued their journey, the path illuminated by the radiant light of their bond. They knew that the challenges they had faced had prepared them for the final trial, and they were ready to retrieve the Shadow Crystal and break the curse.

As they neared their destination, the forest grew darker, the magic more intense. The trees loomed high above them, their branches forming a dense canopy that blocked out the sunlight. The air was thick with tension, and Seraphina could feel the weight of the magic around them.

Finally, they reached a hidden cave, its entrance guarded by a shimmering barrier of energy. The Shadow Crystal lay within, its dark surface pulsing with a malevolent power.

Seraphina and Thorne approached the barrier, their hearts filled with determination. "This is it," Seraphina said, her voice steady. "The final trial."

Thorne nodded. "We must face it together, as we have faced all the challenges before."

They stepped through the barrier, the energy crackling around them. Inside the cave, the Shadow Crystal sat on a pedestal, its dark surface glowing with a sinister light.

As they approached the crystal, they felt a powerful force pulling them closer. The crystal's energy resonated with their own, and they knew that they had to channel their combined magic to retrieve it.

With a deep breath, Seraphina and Thorne began the incantation, their voices harmonizing with the crystal's energy. The cave was filled with a brilliant light as their magic intertwined, forming a radiant force that enveloped the crystal.

The crystal's dark surface began to crack, its malevolent power dissipating. As the incantation reached its climax, the crystal shattered, releasing a surge of energy that filled the cave.

Seraphina and Thorne stood together, their bond and determination stronger than ever. The curse that had bound Thorne for centuries was broken, and the path to their future was clear.

With the Shadow Crystal retrieved and the curse lifted, they returned to the manor, their hearts filled with a sense of accomplishment and purpose. They knew that their journey was far from over, but with their bond and the power of the grimoire, they were ready to face whatever challenges lay ahead.

Together, they would uncover the secrets of the past, fulfill the prophecy, and protect the magical world from destruction. Their bond was unbreakable, their determination unwavering, and their love for each other and their bloodlines a powerful force that would guide them through the darkest of times.

The enchanted forest had tested their resolve and strengthened their bond, and they emerged stronger and more united than ever. As they looked toward the future, they knew that their journey was just beginning, and with each other by their side, there was nothing they could not achieve.

Chapter 4: The Coven's Warning

Seraphina had always felt a deep connection to the coven of Eldergrove. They had been her family, her teachers, and her friends, guiding her through the complexities of magic and the challenges of life as a witch. The Nightshade legacy was intertwined with the coven, and Seraphina's bond with her sisters was strong. However, she knew that her recent actions, especially her association with Thorne, would not go unnoticed or unchallenged.

The morning after their return from the enchanted forest, Seraphina received a summons to the coven's council chamber. The message, delivered by a swift messenger bird, was brief and to the point: "The council requires your presence immediately."

Seraphina sighed, feeling a mixture of anticipation and dread. She had known this moment would come, but she hadn't expected it so soon. She glanced at Thorne, who was seated across the room, studying a newly discovered passage in the grimoire.

"They know," she said simply, her voice tinged with resignation.

Thorne looked up, his eyes meeting hers with concern. "Are you ready for this?"

Seraphina took a deep breath, steeling herself. "I have to be. The coven deserves to know the truth, and I need their support if we're to succeed in our quest."

Thorne nodded, his expression serious. "I'll be here if you need me."

With a final nod, Seraphina left the manor and made her way to the coven's meeting place. The council chamber was located deep within the forest, in a hidden grove that was protected by powerful enchantments. It was a place of great significance, where the coven's most important decisions were made and their deepest secrets guarded.

As she approached the grove, Seraphina felt a sense of unease. The air was thick with tension, and she could sense the energy of the coven members gathered within. She steeled herself and entered the chamber, where she was met by the stern faces of the council.

At the center of the council sat High Priestess Elowen, a wise and powerful witch who had been a mentor to Seraphina for as long as she could remember. Her silver hair and piercing blue eyes gave her an air of authority and wisdom that commanded respect.

"Seraphina," Elowen greeted her, her voice calm but firm. "We have much to discuss."

Seraphina inclined her head in respect. "High Priestess. I understand."

Elowen gestured for her to sit, and Seraphina took her place at the council table. Around her, the other council members watched with a mix of curiosity and concern. Seraphina could feel their scrutiny, their questions hanging in the air like an unspoken challenge.

"Seraphina," Elowen began, "we have learned of your recent activities, particularly your association with the phantom known as Thorne. This news has caused great concern among the coven."

Seraphina nodded, her gaze steady. "I understand your concerns, High Priestess. But I assure you, Thorne is not a threat. He is a victim of a powerful curse, one that I believe we can break together."

Elowen's eyes narrowed slightly. "A phantom is a dangerous entity, Seraphina. Their very nature is one of instability and unpredictability. The risks involved in associating with such a being are immense."

Seraphina took a deep breath, her resolve firm. "I know the risks, High Priestess. But Thorne's curse is intricately tied to our bloodline and the magical world. Breaking it is not just about freeing him; it's about restoring balance and protecting our legacy."

A murmur of voices filled the chamber as the council members exchanged glances. Seraphina could sense the internal conflict, the struggle between caution and the desire to support one of their own.

One of the council members, a stern witch named Morgaine, spoke up. "Seraphina, you must understand that dealing with phantoms has always been fraught with danger. Their existence is often tied to dark magic and malevolent forces. How can we be sure that Thorne's intentions are pure?"

Seraphina met Morgaine's gaze, her voice unwavering. "Thorne's intentions are to break the curse and find peace. He has guided me, protected me, and shared his knowledge to help us uncover the truth. Our bond is strong, and I trust him completely."

Another council member, a younger witch named Aria, spoke with a note of curiosity. "But Seraphina, how did you come to trust him so deeply? What has he done to earn your faith?"

Seraphina recounted their journey into the enchanted forest, the challenges they had faced, and the trials they had overcome together. She spoke of the Rite of Unity, the visions of their ancestors, and the profound connection that had formed between them.

As she spoke, she could see the expressions of the council members shifting, their skepticism giving way to curiosity and a reluctant admiration. They listened intently, their attention focused on her words.

When she finished, there was a moment of silence before Elowen spoke again. "Seraphina, your account is compelling, and it is clear that you have developed a deep bond with Thorne. However, the coven must consider the potential dangers and the broader implications of your actions."

Seraphina nodded, understanding the gravity of the situation. "I am aware of the risks, High Priestess. But I believe that breaking Thorne's curse is not only possible but necessary for the safety and future of our coven and the magical world."

Elowen leaned forward, her gaze piercing. "Seraphina, if we are to support you, we must be certain of your resolve and your ability to handle the consequences. Are you prepared to face whatever challenges may come, even if it means defying the norms of our coven and the magical community?"

Seraphina met Elowen's gaze with unwavering determination. "I am, High Priestess. I will do whatever it takes to break the curse and protect our legacy. Thorne and I are committed to this quest, and I believe we can succeed together."

The council members exchanged glances, the weight of their decision hanging in the air. Finally, Elowen spoke, her voice carrying the authority of her position.

"Very well, Seraphina. The coven will support your quest, but we will do so with caution. You must keep us informed of your progress and any developments. And know that if the situation becomes untenable, we will intervene to protect our coven and the magical world."

Seraphina nodded, her heart filled with gratitude and determination. "Thank you, High Priestess. I will not let you down."

With the council's decision made, Seraphina left the chamber, feeling a mixture of relief and resolve. She knew that the path ahead would be challenging, but with the coven's support and Thorne by her side, she was ready to face whatever trials awaited them.

As Seraphina returned to the manor, she found Thorne waiting for her in the study. His expression was one of concern, but also of hope.

"How did it go?" he asked, his voice gentle.

Seraphina smiled, her heart lightened by the coven's decision. "The council has agreed to support us, but with caution. They understand the risks but also see the potential for our quest to succeed."

Thorne's eyes lit up with relief. "That's good news. With their support, we can move forward with our plans."

Seraphina nodded, her resolve firm. "Yes, but we must be careful. The coven will be watching, and we need to prove that our actions are in the best interest of our legacy and the magical world."

Thorne reached out, taking her hand in his. "We'll do this together, Seraphina. Our bond is strong, and I believe in us."

Seraphina squeezed his hand, feeling a surge of confidence. "I believe in us too, Thorne. Let's continue our quest and uncover the secrets of the grimoire. Together, we can break the curse and restore balance."

With renewed determination, Seraphina and Thorne resumed their study of the grimoire, delving deeper into its mysteries and uncovering new clues about the curse and their bond. Each discovery brought them closer to their goal, and their resolve to succeed grew stronger with each passing day.

The following weeks were a whirlwind of activity as Seraphina and Thorne continued their quest. The grimoire revealed more secrets, each one bringing them closer to understanding the curse and the ancient bond that linked their bloodlines.

One evening, as they pored over a particularly complex passage, Seraphina felt a sudden surge of energy. The grimoire's pages glowed with a brilliant light, and a new section of text appeared before her eyes.

"Thorne, look at this," she said excitedly, pointing to the newly revealed text.

Thorne leaned in, his eyes scanning the words. "This is a revelation spell. It can reveal hidden truths and uncover secrets that have been concealed by powerful magic."

Seraphina's heart raced with excitement. "This could be the key to understanding the full extent of the curse and finding a way to break it."

They quickly gathered the necessary ingredients and prepared to cast the spell. The ritual required them to channel their combined magic into a crystal that would act as a conduit for the revelation spell.

As they began the incantation, the crystal glowed with a radiant light, and a sense of anticipation filled the air. The energy of the spell surged through them, and the room was filled with a brilliant light.

When the spell was complete, the crystal emitted a soft hum, and a vision began to form before them. They saw a time long past, when their ancestors had first forged the Union of Souls. They witnessed the events that had led to the curse, the betrayal of Alaric, and the dark magic that had bound Thorne's spirit.

But there was more. The vision revealed a hidden chamber deep within the enchanted forest, a place where the true origin of the curse was concealed. The chamber was guarded by powerful magic and ancient traps, but within it lay the key to breaking the curse and restoring balance.

Seraphina and Thorne exchanged determined glances. "We need to find that chamber," Seraphina said, her voice filled with resolve. "It's the final piece of the puzzle."

Thorne nodded. "The enchanted forest has tested us before, but with our bond and the support of the coven, we can face whatever challenges lie ahead."

With their path clear, Seraphina and Thorne prepared for their journey to the hidden chamber. They knew that the trials they had faced so far were just the beginning, and the true test of their resolve and determination lay ahead.

As they set off into the forest once more, their hearts were filled with a sense of purpose and hope. The bond that linked them was stronger than ever, and they were ready to face whatever challenges awaited them. Together, they would uncover the secrets of the past, break the curse, and restore balance to the magical world.

Their journey into the enchanted forest was fraught with challenges, each one testing their resolve and strengthening their bond. The forest seemed to sense their purpose, its magic both guiding and challenging them.

One evening, as they camped by a serene lake, Thorne shared more about his past and the curse that had bound him for centuries. He spoke of the pain and isolation he had endured, the moments of hope and despair, and the determination that had kept him going.

Seraphina listened intently, her heart aching for the pain Thorne had endured. "Thorne, I can't imagine what you've been through. But I promise you, we will break this curse and find peace."

Thorne's eyes met hers, filled with gratitude and hope. "Thank you, Seraphina. Your strength and compassion mean more to me than you know."

As the night wore on, they continued their study of the grimoire, uncovering more clues about the hidden chamber and the trials that awaited them. Each discovery brought them closer to their goal, and their resolve to succeed grew stronger with each passing day.

Finally, after weeks of travel and trials, they reached the entrance to the hidden chamber. The entrance was concealed by powerful enchantments, but with their combined magic, they were able to reveal the way forward.

As they entered the chamber, they were met by a series of challenges designed to test their intelligence, strength, and determination. The chamber was filled with ancient traps and guardians, each one more formidable than the last.

But Seraphina and Thorne faced each challenge with unwavering resolve, their bond and determination guiding their actions. They worked together seamlessly, their trust in each other unbreakable.

Finally, they reached the heart of the chamber, where the true origin of the curse was revealed. The chamber was filled with a dark, malevolent energy, and at its center lay a powerful artifact—the Heart of Shadows.

The Heart of Shadows pulsed with a dark energy, its surface swirling with malevolent power. Seraphina and Thorne knew that breaking the curse would require them to confront this dark force and harness its power.

With a deep breath, Seraphina and Thorne began the final incantation, their voices harmonizing with the dark energy of the Heart of Shadows. The chamber was filled with a brilliant light as their magic intertwined, forming a radiant force that enveloped the artifact.

The dark energy of the Heart of Shadows began to dissipate, its malevolent power unraveling. As the incantation reached its climax, the artifact shattered, releasing a surge of energy that filled the chamber.

Seraphina and Thorne stood together, their bond and determination stronger than ever. The curse that had bound Thorne for centuries was broken, and the path to their future was clear.

With the Heart of Shadows destroyed and the curse lifted, they returned to the manor, their hearts filled with a sense of accomplishment and purpose. They knew that their journey was far from over, but with their bond and the power of the grimoire, they were ready to face whatever challenges lay ahead.

Back at the manor, the coven awaited their return, their faces filled with a mixture of anticipation and concern. High Priestess Elowen stepped forward, her eyes searching Seraphina's for answers.

"Seraphina," Elowen said, her voice calm but filled with curiosity, "have you succeeded in your quest?"

Seraphina nodded, her heart lightened by their success. "Yes, High Priestess. We have uncovered the true origin of the curse and destroyed the Heart of Shadows. Thorne is free, and the curse is broken."

A murmur of approval and relief swept through the coven, and Elowen's eyes softened with pride. "You have proven yourself, Seraphina. Your determination and strength have guided you through the trials, and you have succeeded where many would have failed."

Seraphina felt a surge of gratitude and pride. "Thank you, High Priestess. I could not have done it without the support of the coven and the bond I share with Thorne."

Elowen nodded, her gaze filled with wisdom. "The bond you share is a testament to the power of unity and determination. It is a reminder that even in the face of darkness and uncertainty, the strength of our connections can guide us through."

With the coven's approval and support, Seraphina and Thorne knew that their journey was just beginning. The challenges they had faced had strengthened their bond and prepared them for the trials ahead. Together, they would continue to uncover the secrets of the past, protect their legacy, and forge a new future.

As they looked toward the horizon, their hearts filled with hope and determination, they knew that the path before them was filled with challenges and opportunities. But with their bond and the power of the grimoire, they were ready to face whatever lay ahead. Their journey was far from over, and with each other by their side, there was nothing they could not achieve.

The coven's warning had tested their resolve, but it had also strengthened their determination. With the support of their sisters and the bond they shared, Seraphina and Thorne were ready to face the future, knowing that together, they could overcome any obstacle and protect the magical world they loved.

Chapter 5: The Phantom's Past

The fire crackled softly in the hearth of the Nightshade manor's study, casting flickering shadows on the walls. The warmth of the flames was a stark contrast to the chill that seemed to linger in the air, a reminder of the dark magic that had bound Thorne for centuries. Seraphina and Thorne sat together, the grimoire open on the table before them, its ancient pages filled with secrets yet to be fully uncovered.

Seraphina glanced at Thorne, who was staring into the fire, his expression distant and thoughtful. She could sense that he was wrestling with memories from his past, memories that were painful and difficult to share. She reached out and placed a hand on his arm, offering silent support.

"Thorne," she said gently, "I know that sharing your past is difficult, but I believe it's important for us to understand what happened. It will help us break the curse and restore balance."

Thorne's gaze shifted from the fire to Seraphina's eyes, and he gave a small nod. "You're right, Seraphina. It's time you knew the full story."

He took a deep breath, gathering his thoughts, and began to speak, his voice filled with a mixture of sorrow and determination.

In a time long past, in a land far from Eldergrove, Thorne had been a powerful sorcerer, renowned for his mastery of the arcane arts. His family, the Blackthornes, had been respected and revered for generations, their lineage steeped in magic and mystery. Thorne had shown a natural talent for magic from a young age, and his parents had nurtured his abilities, providing him with the best education and training.

As a young man, Thorne had quickly risen to prominence, his skills surpassing even the most experienced sorcerers. He had been ambitious and driven, eager to unlock the secrets of the universe and push the boundaries of magical knowledge. His thirst for power had led him to seek out ancient tomes and artifacts, delving into forbidden realms and experimenting with dark magic.

It was during this time that Thorne had met Alaric, a fellow sorcerer who shared his ambition and drive. Alaric had been charismatic and persuasive, and the two had quickly formed an alliance, pooling their knowledge and resources to achieve their goals. Together, they had embarked on a quest to uncover the secrets of immortality, believing that such power would elevate them to godlike status.

For years, Thorne and Alaric had worked tirelessly, their bond growing stronger as they faced countless challenges and dangers. They had uncovered ancient scrolls, deciphered cryptic runes, and performed powerful rituals, each step bringing them closer to their ultimate goal. Thorne had trusted Alaric completely, viewing him as a brother and confidant.

But as their power grew, so did Alaric's envy and greed. Thorne's natural talent and rapid progress had begun to overshadow Alaric's achievements, and jealousy had taken root in Alaric's heart. Unbeknownst to Thorne, Alaric had begun to plot against him, seeking a way to eliminate his rival and claim the power for himself.

The betrayal had come swiftly and without warning. One night, as Thorne and Alaric performed a particularly complex ritual, Alaric had seized the opportunity to strike. Using a powerful curse that he had secretly crafted, Alaric had bound Thorne's spirit to the mortal world, trapping him in a state of eternal limbo. Thorne had been rendered a phantom, unable to die but also unable to truly live.

The shock and pain of the betrayal had been overwhelming. Thorne had trusted Alaric with his life, and that trust had been shattered in an instant. As he struggled to come to terms with his new existence, Thorne had vowed to find a way to break the curse and seek justice for the wrongs that had been done to him.

AS THORNE RECOUNTED his story, Seraphina listened intently, her heart aching for the pain he had endured. She could see the depth of his sorrow and the weight of the betrayal that had shaped his existence. Despite the darkness of his past, she felt a growing admiration for Thorne's strength and resilience.

"Thorne," she said softly, "I can't imagine the pain you've been through. But I promise you, we will find a way to break this curse and bring Alaric to justice."

Thorne's eyes met hers, filled with gratitude and hope. "Thank you, Seraphina. Your belief in me means more than you know. Together, we can overcome this."

Seraphina felt a deep connection to Thorne, a bond that transcended time and space. She knew that their journey would be challenging, but with their combined strength and determination, they could succeed.

"Tell me more about your life before the curse," Seraphina said, wanting to understand Thorne's past more fully. "What were your dreams and aspirations?"

Thorne's expression softened as he recalled his early years. "I grew up in a family of powerful sorcerers. My parents were kind and wise, and they nurtured my talents from a young age. I was always curious and eager to learn, and my greatest ambition was to unlock the secrets of the universe. I believed that with enough knowledge and power, I could achieve anything."

He paused, a wistful smile playing on his lips. "I had a sister, Elara. She was my best friend and confidante. We shared a special bond, and she was always there to support me, no matter what. Losing her was the hardest part of all this."

Seraphina's heart went out to Thorne. "I'm so sorry, Thorne. It sounds like you had a close and loving family."

Thorne nodded, his eyes filled with a mixture of sorrow and fondness. "Yes, we were close. My family meant everything to me. When I was cursed, I lost not only my physical form but also my connection to them. I was forced to watch them from afar, unable to interact or protect them."

Seraphina could feel the depth of Thorne's pain and the weight of the centuries he had spent as a phantom. She reached out and took his hand, offering silent support.

"We will break this curse, Thorne," she said with determination. "And when we do, you'll be able to find peace and reconnect with your family, even if it's only in spirit."

Thorne squeezed her hand, his eyes filled with gratitude. "Thank you, Seraphina. Your strength and compassion give me hope that we can succeed."

As the night wore on, Thorne continued to share more about his past life, painting a vivid picture of the world he had once known. He spoke of his studies in the arcane arts, his adventures with Alaric, and the moments of joy and sorrow that had defined his existence.

Seraphina listened with rapt attention, her heart growing heavier with each revelation. She could see the depth of Thorne's character, his resilience in the face of unimaginable adversity, and his unwavering determination to find justice and peace.

One particularly poignant memory stood out. Thorne recounted a time when he and Alaric had ventured into a forbidden realm in search of a powerful artifact. The journey had been fraught with danger, and they had faced numerous trials that tested their skills and their bond.

"Alaric and I were like brothers," Thorne said, his voice filled with a mixture of nostalgia and bitterness. "We trusted each other completely, and I believed that our bond was unbreakable. But I was blind to his growing jealousy and ambition. I didn't see the betrayal coming until it was too late."

Seraphina could feel the weight of Thorne's words, the pain of a friendship that had been shattered by betrayal. She reached out and placed a comforting hand on his shoulder.

"Thorne, you were betrayed by someone you trusted deeply. It's natural to feel anger and sorrow, but you have shown incredible strength in the face of that betrayal. You are not defined by Alaric's actions. You are defined by your resilience and your determination to find justice."

Thorne looked at Seraphina, his eyes filled with gratitude and admiration. "Thank you, Seraphina. Your words mean more to me than you know. With you by my side, I believe that we can break this curse and find the peace I've longed for."

Seraphina felt a deep connection to Thorne, a bond that had grown stronger with each passing day. She knew that their journey was far from over, but with their combined strength and determination, they could face whatever challenges lay ahead.

As the first light of dawn began to filter through the windows, Seraphina and Thorne continued to delve into the grimoire, uncovering more clues about the curse and the ancient bond that linked their bloodlines. Each discovery brought them closer to understanding the full extent of the curse and finding a way to break it.

One particularly revealing passage described a ritual known as the Rite of Redemption. This powerful ceremony had the potential to cleanse a soul of dark magic and restore balance to the spirit. The ritual required the caster to confront the source of the curse directly and perform a series of complex incantations.

"This could be the key to breaking the curse," Seraphina said, her voice filled with excitement. "The Rite of Redemption might be exactly what we need."

Thorne nodded, his expression serious. "But it's not without risks. Confronting the source of the curse will require us to face Alaric and the dark magic he wielded. We must be prepared for whatever challenges lie ahead."

Seraphina's resolve was unwavering. "We can do this, Thorne. With our bond and the support of the coven, we have the

strength to succeed."

Thorne's eyes met hers, filled with determination and hope. "Together, we can overcome anything."

As they prepared for the ritual, Seraphina felt a growing sense of purpose and connection to Thorne. She knew that their journey would be challenging, but with their combined strength and determination, they could break the curse and restore balance to their bloodlines.

The day of the Rite of Redemption dawned clear and bright, a stark contrast to the darkness they were about to face. Seraphina and Thorne made their way to a secluded glade in the enchanted forest, a place of great power and significance. The air was filled with anticipation, and Seraphina could feel the weight of their task pressing down on her.

As they reached the center of the glade, they began to prepare the ritual. The Rite of Redemption required a series of intricate symbols and runes to be inscribed on the ground, along with a circle of enchanted candles to channel their magic.

Seraphina and Thorne worked together, their movements synchronized and their bond guiding their actions. As they completed the preparations, they took their places at the center of the circle, their hands clasped together.

With a deep breath, Seraphina began the incantation, her voice steady and filled with power. "By the power of the Union of Souls, we call upon the spirits of our ancestors. Grant us the strength and wisdom to confront the darkness and restore balance to our bloodlines."

Thorne joined her, his voice resonant with determination. "By the bond that links us, we seek to cleanse our souls of dark magic and break the curse that binds us. Let the light of redemption shine upon us and guide us through the darkness."

As they chanted, the air around them shimmered with a brilliant light, and the ground beneath their feet seemed to pulse with energy. The candles flared to life, their flames dancing with an ethereal glow.

Suddenly, the air grew cold, and a dark presence filled the glade. A figure emerged from the shadows, its form twisted and malevolent. Alaric's spirit stood before them, his eyes burning with hatred and jealousy.

"You dare to challenge me?" Alaric sneered, his voice filled with venom. "You will find that the power of the curse is beyond your comprehension."

Seraphina met Alaric's gaze with unwavering resolve. "We will break the curse, Alaric. Your reign of terror ends today."

A battle of wills ensued, the air crackling with magical energy as Seraphina and Thorne confronted Alaric. The dark sorcerer's power was formidable, but Seraphina and Thorne's bond and determination proved to be a match for him.

With a final surge of energy, they completed the Rite of Redemption, their combined magic enveloping Alaric's spirit and cleansing it of dark magic. The malevolent presence dissipated, and the glade was filled with a brilliant light.

Seraphina and Thorne stood together, their bond stronger than ever. The curse that had bound Thorne for centuries was broken, and the path to their future was clear.

With the Rite of Redemption complete, they returned to the manor, their hearts filled with a sense of accomplishment and purpose. They knew that their journey was far from over, but with their bond and the power of the grimoire, they were ready to face whatever challenges lay ahead.

Back at the manor, the coven awaited their return, their faces filled with a mixture of anticipation and concern. High Priestess Elowen stepped forward, her eyes searching Seraphina's for answers.

"Seraphina," Elowen said, her voice calm but filled with curiosity, "have you succeeded in your quest?"

Seraphina nodded, her heart lightened by their success. "Yes, High Priestess. We have broken the curse and cleansed our souls of dark magic. Thorne is free, and the path to our future is clear."

A murmur of approval and relief swept through the coven, and Elowen's eyes softened with pride. "You have proven yourselves, Seraphina and Thorne. Your determination and strength have guided you through the trials, and you have succeeded where many would have failed."

Seraphina felt a surge of gratitude and pride. "Thank you, High Priestess. I could not have done it without the support of the coven and the bond I share with Thorne."

Elowen nodded, her gaze filled with wisdom. "The bond you share is a testament to the power of unity and determination. It is a reminder that even in the face of darkness and uncertainty, the strength of our connections can guide us through."

With the coven's approval and support, Seraphina and Thorne knew that their journey was just beginning. The challenges they had faced had strengthened their bond and prepared them for the trials ahead. Together, they would continue to uncover the secrets of the past, protect their legacy, and forge a new future.

As they looked toward the horizon, their hearts filled with hope and determination, they knew that the path before them was filled with challenges and opportunities. But with their bond and the power of the grimoire, they were ready to face whatever lay ahead. Their journey was far from over, and with each other by their side, there was nothing they could not achieve.

In the days that followed, Seraphina and Thorne continued to delve into the grimoire, uncovering more secrets about their ancestors and the magical world. They discovered ancient spells and rituals that had been lost to time, each one bringing them closer to understanding the full extent of their bond and the power they possessed.

One evening, as they studied a particularly complex incantation, Thorne turned to Seraphina, his eyes filled with a mixture of curiosity and admiration. "Seraphina, do you ever wonder what our lives would have been like if the curse had never happened?"

Seraphina considered his question, her heart filled with a sense of longing and possibility. "I do, Thorne. I think about it often. But I also believe that everything happens for a reason. Our bond and our journey have shaped us into who we are today."

Thorne nodded, a thoughtful smile playing on his lips. "You're right. Our experiences have made us stronger and more resilient. And now, we have the chance to shape our own future."

Seraphina felt a deep sense of connection to Thorne, a bond that transcended time and space. She knew that their journey was far from over, but with their combined strength and determination, they could face whatever challenges lay ahead.

"Let's continue our study of the grimoire," Seraphina said, her voice filled with resolve. "There is still much to learn, and our journey is just beginning."

Thorne's eyes met hers, filled with determination and hope. "Together, we can uncover the secrets of the past and forge a new future."

As they delved deeper into the grimoire, Seraphina felt a growing sense of purpose and connection to Thorne. She knew that their bond was a powerful force, one that could guide them through the darkest of times and help them achieve their greatest aspirations.

With each discovery, their resolve grew stronger, and their determination to protect their legacy and the magical world was unwavering. Together, they would continue to uncover the secrets of the past, break the curses that bound them, and forge a new future filled with hope and possibility.

Their journey was far from over, but with their bond and the power of the grimoire, there was nothing they could not achieve. Seraphina and Thorne were ready to face whatever challenges lay ahead, knowing that together, they could overcome any obstacle and protect the magical world they loved.

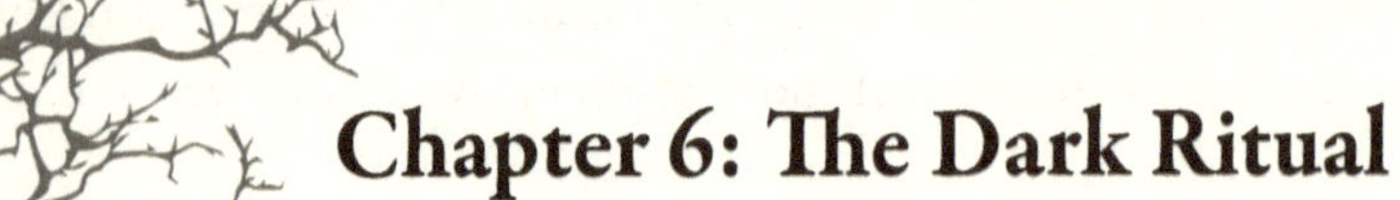

Chapter 6: The Dark Ritual

The moon hung high in the night sky, casting a silvery glow over the dense forest that surrounded the Nightshade manor. Inside the manor, the atmosphere was charged with anticipation and a hint of unease. Seraphina and Thorne had spent weeks delving into the grimoire, uncovering ancient spells and hidden secrets, but tonight, they were about to undertake their most dangerous endeavor yet: the Dark Ritual.

The Dark Ritual was a powerful incantation that promised to unveil more secrets of the grimoire, potentially revealing an ancient prophecy that could change the course of the magical world. It was a ritual shrouded in mystery and danger, its origins lost to time. The grimoire warned of the risks involved, but it also hinted at the incredible knowledge and power that could be gained.

Seraphina stood in the study, her heart pounding with a mix of excitement and trepidation. The room was prepared for the ritual, the air thick with the scent of rare herbs and the flickering light of black candles casting eerie shadows on the walls. At the center of the room lay a large, ornate circle inscribed with intricate runes and symbols, meticulously drawn with a mixture of blood and crushed gemstones.

Thorne entered the room, his expression serious and focused. He had spent the day gathering the final ingredients for the ritual, and now everything was ready.

"Are you sure about this, Seraphina?" Thorne asked, his voice tinged with concern. "The Dark Ritual is incredibly dangerous. There's no telling what consequences it might bring."

Seraphina met his gaze, her resolve unwavering. "I know the risks, Thorne. But we need to uncover the truth behind the prophecy and the secrets of the grimoire. This ritual is our best chance."

Thorne nodded, his expression softening with admiration. "Very well. Let's proceed with caution."

Together, they stepped into the circle, their hands clasped together. Seraphina took a deep breath and began to chant the incantation, her voice steady and filled with power. Thorne joined her, their voices harmonizing as they channeled their magic into the runes and symbols.

The air around them shimmered with a dark energy, and the temperature in the room seemed to drop. The candles flickered wildly, and the symbols on the floor began to glow with an otherworldly light. As the incantation reached its climax, a surge of energy pulsed through the room, and the ground beneath their feet seemed to tremble.

Suddenly, the air was filled with a blinding light, and a vision began to form before them. They saw a time long past, a world filled with magic and wonder. In the vision, a powerful witch and a phantom stood side by side, their bond and combined magic changing the course of history. They fought against dark forces, their strength and determination guiding them through countless trials and tribulations.

As the vision continued, Seraphina and Thorne saw themselves in the place of the witch and phantom, their bond and power mirroring the ancient figures. The vision revealed an ancient prophecy, one that spoke of a witch and a phantom destined to change the magical world, to bring balance and protect it from the forces of darkness.

The vision faded, and Seraphina and Thorne found themselves back in the study, their hearts racing with the weight of what they had seen. The prophecy was clear: they were destined to play a crucial role in the fate of the magical world.

Before they could fully process the revelation, the ground beneath them shook violently, and a chilling wind swept through the room. The dark energy of the ritual had attracted the attention of malevolent forces, drawn by the power and significance of the prophecy.

The room was filled with a sinister presence, and Seraphina and Thorne could feel the weight of the dark forces pressing down on them. Shadows seemed to come alive, their shapes twisting and writhing as they moved closer.

"We need to protect ourselves," Thorne said urgently, his eyes scanning the room for any sign of an attack.

Seraphina nodded, her mind racing. She quickly began to chant a protective spell, her voice filled with determination. Thorne joined her, their combined magic forming a barrier of light around them.

The shadows hissed and recoiled from the light, but they did not retreat. The dark forces were relentless, their malevolent energy growing stronger with each passing moment.

"We can't hold them off forever," Thorne warned, his voice strained with the effort of maintaining the barrier. "We need to find a way to banish them."

Seraphina's mind raced, searching for a solution. She remembered a banishment spell she had read in the grimoire, a powerful incantation that could drive away dark forces. With a deep breath, she began to chant the spell, her voice filled with authority and power.

Thorne joined her, their voices merging into a harmonious chant that echoed through the room. The barrier of light around them intensified, and the shadows began to waver and retreat.

With a final surge of energy, the banishment spell reached its climax, and the dark forces were driven from the room. The air cleared, and the oppressive presence lifted, leaving Seraphina and Thorne standing in the study, their hearts still racing.

"We did it," Seraphina said, her voice filled with relief.

Thorne nodded, his expression serious. "But the ritual has set something in motion. The dark forces will not give up easily. We need to be prepared for whatever comes next."

Seraphina took a deep breath, her resolve strengthening. "The prophecy has revealed our destiny, Thorne. We must continue our quest and protect the magical world from the darkness. Together, we can face whatever challenges lie ahead."

Thorne's eyes met hers, filled with determination and hope. "Together, we can overcome anything."

With their bond stronger than ever and the revelation of the prophecy guiding their actions, Seraphina and Thorne knew that their journey was far from over. The Dark Ritual had unveiled powerful secrets and set them on a path filled with danger and uncertainty, but they were ready to face whatever challenges lay ahead.

In the days that followed, Seraphina and Thorne continued to study the grimoire, seeking to uncover more about the prophecy and the dark forces that threatened the magical world. The revelation of the prophecy had given them a sense of purpose and direction, but it had also attracted the attention of malevolent entities that sought to thwart their efforts.

The coven, having learned of the ritual and its consequences, rallied around Seraphina and Thorne, offering their support and resources. High Priestess Elowen, ever wise and vigilant, took a personal interest in their quest, providing guidance and counsel.

"Seraphina, Thorne," Elowen said one evening as they gathered in the council chamber, "the prophecy you have uncovered is of great significance. It speaks of a time when the magical world will face its greatest challenge, and you two are destined to play a crucial role in its defense. But with this knowledge comes great danger. The dark forces will stop at nothing to prevent the prophecy from coming to fruition."

Seraphina nodded, her resolve firm. "We understand the risks, High Priestess. But we are committed to this quest. We will do whatever it takes to protect the magical world and fulfill our destiny."

Thorne's eyes met Elowen's, filled with determination. "We have faced many challenges already, and our bond has only grown stronger. We are ready to face whatever comes next."

Elowen's expression softened with approval. "Very well. The coven will continue to support you in your efforts. But be cautious. The dark forces are cunning and relentless. Trust in each other and in the strength of your bond."

With the coven's support and the guidance of the prophecy, Seraphina and Thorne continued their quest, delving deeper into the grimoire and uncovering more secrets about the ancient magic that bound them.

One evening, as they studied a particularly complex passage in the grimoire, Seraphina felt a sudden surge of energy. The pages seemed to come alive, the words shifting and rearranging themselves before her eyes.

"Thorne, look at this," she said, her voice filled with excitement. "The grimoire is revealing more about the prophecy."

Thorne leaned in, his eyes scanning the newly revealed text. "It speaks of a powerful artifact, the Celestial Amulet. It is said to hold the key to unlocking the full potential of the prophecy and protecting the magical world from the dark forces."

Seraphina's heart raced with excitement. "We need to find this amulet. It could be the key to fulfilling our destiny."

Thorne nodded, his expression serious. "But the amulet is likely well-guarded. We must be prepared for whatever challenges lie ahead."

With their path clear, Seraphina and Thorne began to prepare for their journey to find the Celestial Amulet. The grimoire provided clues about its location, leading them to believe that it was hidden in a remote and treacherous region known as the Shadowlands.

The Shadowlands were a place of great danger, filled with dark magic and malevolent creatures. But Seraphina and Thorne knew that they had to face these challenges head-on if they were to find the amulet and fulfill the prophecy.

As they set off on their journey, the air was filled with a sense of anticipation and determination. The path ahead was fraught with danger, but Seraphina and Thorne were ready to face whatever challenges lay ahead. Their bond was strong, and their resolve unwavering.

The journey to the Shadowlands was long and arduous, filled with numerous challenges and trials. The landscape was harsh and unforgiving, with treacherous terrain and powerful magical barriers that tested their skills and determination.

As they ventured deeper into the Shadowlands, the air grew thick with a dark energy, and the presence of malevolent forces became more palpable. Seraphina and Thorne encountered dark creatures and powerful sorcerers, each one more formidable than the last.

One evening, as they made camp in a small clearing, Thorne shared more about his past and the events that had led to his curse. The firelight danced on his face, casting shadows that seemed to mirror the darkness of his memories.

"I was once a powerful sorcerer, renowned for my mastery of the arcane arts," Thorne began, his voice filled with a mixture of sorrow and determination. "But my ambition led me down a dangerous path. I sought to unlock the secrets of immortality, believing that such power would elevate me to godlike status. Alaric, a fellow sorcerer, shared my ambition, and we formed an alliance to achieve our goals."

Seraphina listened intently, her heart aching for the pain Thorne had endured. "What happened, Thorne? How did you come to be cursed?"

Thorne's expression darkened. "As our power grew, so did Alaric's envy and greed. He began to see me as a rival, a threat to his own ambitions. One night, as we performed a particularly complex ritual, Alaric betrayed me. He used a powerful curse to bind my spirit to the mortal world, trapping me in a state of eternal limbo. I became a phantom, unable to die but also unable to truly live."

Seraphina reached out and placed a comforting hand on Thorne's shoulder. "I'm so sorry, Thorne. You were betrayed by someone you trusted deeply. But we will break this curse and find justice for the wrongs that were done to you."

Thorne's eyes met hers, filled with gratitude and hope. "Thank you, Seraphina. With you by my side, I believe that we can succeed."

Their bond had grown stronger with each passing day, and Seraphina felt a deep connection to Thorne, one that transcended time and space. She knew that their journey was far from over, but with their combined strength and determination, they could face whatever challenges lay ahead.

As they continued their journey, Seraphina and Thorne encountered numerous challenges that tested their skills and their bond. They faced dark creatures and powerful sorcerers, each one more formidable than the last. But with each trial, their bond grew stronger, and their determination to succeed never wavered.

One particularly challenging encounter occurred when they were ambushed by a group of dark sorcerers, led by a powerful mage named Malachai. The sorcerers had been sent by the dark forces to thwart Seraphina and Thorne's efforts and prevent them from finding the Celestial Amulet.

The battle was fierce and relentless, the air crackling with magical energy as spells clashed and collided. Seraphina and Thorne fought with all their might, their bond guiding their movements and their magic intertwining in a harmonious dance.

Despite the formidable power of their adversaries, Seraphina and Thorne's bond and determination proved to be a match for them. With a final surge of energy, they managed to defeat Malachai and his followers, driving them from the Shadowlands.

"We did it," Seraphina said, her voice filled with relief and triumph.

Thorne nodded, his expression serious. "But the dark forces will not give up easily. We must remain vigilant and continue our quest."

With the threat of Malachai and his followers behind them, Seraphina and Thorne continued their journey, their hearts filled with a sense of purpose and hope. They knew that the path ahead was filled with challenges, but they were ready to face whatever lay ahead.

After weeks of travel and trials, they finally reached the heart of the Shadowlands, where the Celestial Amulet was said to be hidden. The landscape was stark and desolate, the air thick with a palpable sense of darkness and foreboding.

At the center of the desolate landscape stood an ancient temple, its walls covered in intricate runes and symbols. The temple was well-guarded, its entrance protected by powerful enchantments and malevolent creatures.

Seraphina and Thorne approached the temple with caution, their senses on high alert. They knew that obtaining the Celestial Amulet would not be easy, and they had to be prepared for whatever challenges lay ahead.

As they reached the entrance, Seraphina began to chant a series of incantations, her voice steady and filled with power. The runes on the temple walls glowed with an otherworldly light, and the protective enchantments began to weaken.

With a final surge of energy, the enchantments were broken, and the entrance to the temple opened before them. Seraphina and Thorne entered the temple, their hearts filled with anticipation and determination.

Inside, the temple was filled with ancient artifacts and powerful relics, each one exuding a sense of magic and history. At the center of the temple lay the Celestial Amulet, its surface shimmering with a radiant light.

As they approached the amulet, a powerful force filled the room, and the air crackled with energy. The amulet's magic resonated with their own, and they knew that they had to channel their combined power to retrieve it.

With a deep breath, Seraphina and Thorne began the incantation, their voices harmonizing with the amulet's energy. The air around them shimmered with a brilliant light, and the ground beneath their feet seemed to tremble.

Suddenly, the room was filled with a blinding light, and a vision began to form before them. They saw the ancient prophecy once more, the witch and the phantom standing side by side, their bond and combined magic changing the course of history.

The vision revealed more about their destiny, the challenges they would face, and the role they were destined to play in protecting the magical world from the forces of darkness. The prophecy was clear: their bond and determination were the key to unlocking the full potential of the prophecy and fulfilling their destiny.

As the vision faded, Seraphina and Thorne found themselves back in the temple, the Celestial Amulet in their hands. The amulet's magic pulsed with a radiant light, and they knew that they had unlocked a powerful tool in their quest to protect the magical world.

With the Celestial Amulet in their possession, they made their way back to the manor, their hearts filled with a sense of accomplishment and purpose. They knew that their journey was far from over, but with the amulet and the support of the coven, they were ready to face whatever challenges lay ahead.

BACK AT THE MANOR, the coven awaited their return, their faces filled with a mixture of anticipation and concern. High Priestess Elowen stepped forward, her eyes searching Seraphina's for answers.

"Seraphina, Thorne," Elowen said, her voice calm but filled with curiosity, "have you succeeded in your quest?"

Seraphina nodded, her heart lightened by their success. "Yes, High Priestess. We have found the Celestial Amulet and unlocked more secrets of the prophecy. The amulet holds the key to protecting the magical world from the dark forces."

A murmur of approval and relief swept through the coven, and Elowen's eyes softened with pride. "You have proven yourselves once more. Your determination and strength have guided you through the trials, and you have succeeded where many would have failed."

Seraphina felt a surge of gratitude and pride. "Thank you, High Priestess. I could not have done it without the support of the coven and the bond I share with Thorne."

Elowen nodded, her gaze filled with wisdom. "The bond you share is a testament to the power of unity and determination. It is a reminder that even in the face of darkness and uncertainty, the strength of our connections can guide us through."

With the coven's approval and support, Seraphina and Thorne knew that their journey was just beginning. The challenges they had faced had strengthened their bond and prepared them for the trials ahead. Together, they would continue to uncover the secrets of the past, protect their legacy, and forge a new future.

As they looked toward the horizon, their hearts filled with hope and determination, they knew that the path before them was filled with challenges and opportunities. But with their bond and the power of the grimoire, they were ready to face whatever lay ahead. Their journey was far from over, and with each other by their side, there was nothing they could not achieve.

The Dark Ritual had unveiled powerful secrets and set them on a path filled with danger and uncertainty, but Seraphina and Thorne were ready to face whatever challenges lay ahead. Their bond was unbreakable, their determination unwavering, and their love for each other and their bloodlines a powerful force that would guide them through the darkest of times.

Chapter 7: The Shadow Realm

The sun had long set, casting the Nightshade manor in a cloak of darkness. Seraphina and Thorne were preparing for their most perilous journey yet: a venture into the Shadow Realm. The ancient grimoire, with its cryptic instructions, had revealed that the Shadow Realm held crucial information about the prophecy that bound their fates. The Celestial Amulet, now glowing softly in Seraphina's hands, was to be their guide and protector in that forbidding place.

As they made their final preparations in the study, the weight of their task loomed over them. Thorne's eyes met Seraphina's, reflecting both determination and a hint of concern.

"Are you ready for this?" Thorne asked, his voice low but steady.

Seraphina nodded, her resolve unwavering. "We have to be. The answers we seek are in the Shadow Realm, and we can't turn back now."

With the grimoire open to the page detailing the incantation for entering the Shadow Realm, Seraphina began to chant. Her voice, infused with power, filled the room. Thorne joined her, their voices blending in perfect harmony. The air around them shimmered with dark energy, and the Celestial Amulet's light intensified, casting a protective glow over them.

As the incantation reached its climax, a portal of swirling shadows and light opened before them. Taking a deep breath, Seraphina and Thorne stepped through the portal, leaving the familiar world behind and entering the enigmatic Shadow Realm.

THE SHADOW REALM WAS a place of perpetual twilight, where shadows seemed to possess a life of their own. The air was thick with a cold, oppressive energy, and the landscape was a desolate expanse of jagged rocks and twisted trees. Seraphina and Thorne emerged from the portal onto a rocky outcrop, the portal closing behind them with a whisper of dark magic.

The Celestial Amulet glowed brightly, casting a protective aura around them. Seraphina clutched it tightly, feeling its warmth and power.

"This place feels... wrong," Thorne said, his eyes scanning the dark horizon. "We need to stay alert. The Shadow Realm is filled with dangers."

Seraphina nodded, her senses heightened. "Let's move quickly and find the information we need."

They began their journey through the Shadow Realm, the amulet's light guiding their path. As they ventured deeper, the shadows seemed to grow thicker, their forms shifting and writhing like living entities. The air was filled with eerie whispers, as if the shadows were communicating with one another.

Suddenly, a shadowy figure darted towards them, its form indistinct and malevolent. Seraphina and Thorne reacted instinctively, their combined magic forming a barrier of light that repelled the creature. The shadow hissed and retreated, merging back into the darkness.

"That was too close," Seraphina said, her heart pounding.

Thorne nodded, his expression grim. "We need to be more careful. The creatures here are drawn to our light."

They continued their journey, encountering more shadow creatures along the way. Each battle tested their skills and their bond, but they fought with unwavering determination, their combined magic a beacon of hope in the dark realm.

After what felt like hours of navigating the treacherous landscape, they came upon a massive, ancient structure. The building was made of dark stone, its architecture both alien and foreboding. The Celestial Amulet's light seemed to pulse with renewed intensity, indicating that they were close to their destination.

"This must be the place," Seraphina said, her voice filled with a mix of awe and apprehension.

Thorne nodded. "Let's find out what secrets it holds."

As they approached the entrance, they were met by a powerful force field that blocked their path. The field crackled with dark energy, impenetrable by conventional means. Seraphina and Thorne exchanged determined glances, knowing that they would need to use their combined magic to breach it.

With a deep breath, they began to chant an incantation, their voices merging in a harmonious blend of power. The Celestial Amulet's light intensified, and a beam of pure energy shot towards the force field. The dark energy crackled and resisted, but their combined power proved stronger. With a final surge of magic, the force field shattered, allowing them entry.

Inside, the air was thick with an ancient, oppressive energy. The interior was vast and dimly lit, with towering columns and intricate carvings that seemed to tell a story long forgotten. Seraphina and Thorne moved cautiously, their senses on high alert.

As they ventured deeper into the structure, they heard a faint, melodic hum. The sound grew louder as they approached a grand chamber, at the center of which stood a figure cloaked in shadows. The figure's presence exuded a powerful, enigmatic energy, and Seraphina could sense that this was the guardian they had been seeking.

"Welcome, seekers," the guardian said, its voice resonating with a strange, ethereal quality. "I have been expecting you."

Seraphina and Thorne exchanged wary glances before stepping forward. "We seek answers about the prophecy and the curse that binds us," Seraphina said, her voice steady.

The guardian nodded, its form shifting slightly in the dim light. "You are destined to play a crucial role in the fate of the magical world. The prophecy speaks of a witch and a phantom whose bond and combined power will bring balance and protect against the forces of darkness."

Thorne stepped closer, his eyes filled with determination. "What do we need to do to fulfill the prophecy and break the curse?"

The guardian's form seemed to solidify, and it extended a shadowy hand towards them. "To understand the prophecy and the curse, you must first understand the origin of the dark forces that seek to destroy you. The curse that binds you was cast by a powerful sorcerer, driven by envy and greed. His spirit still lingers in the Shadow Realm, seeking to thwart your efforts and claim the power of the prophecy for himself."

Seraphina's heart pounded with a mix of fear and resolve. "How can we confront and defeat this sorcerer?"

The guardian's voice took on a grave tone. "The sorcerer's spirit is bound to a powerful artifact known as the Shadow Core. To break the curse and fulfill the prophecy, you must locate and destroy the Shadow Core. But be warned, the sorcerer will do everything in his power to stop you."

Thorne's eyes burned with determination. "We will face whatever challenges come our way. Together, we are stronger."

The guardian nodded approvingly. "Your bond is your greatest strength. Trust in each other and in the light of the Celestial Amulet. It will guide you through the darkness."

With the guardian's words echoing in their minds, Seraphina and Thorne set off to find the Shadow Core. The path ahead was fraught with danger, but their determination was unwavering.

As they ventured deeper into the Shadow Realm, the landscape grew more twisted and treacherous. The shadows seemed to grow thicker and more aggressive, and the air was filled with an oppressive energy that weighed heavily on their spirits.

Seraphina clutched the Celestial Amulet tightly, its light a beacon of hope in the dark realm. "We must be close. The shadows are growing stronger."

Thorne nodded, his eyes scanning the horizon. "Stay alert. The sorcerer will likely try to stop us before we reach the Shadow Core."

Their journey led them to a massive, ancient fortress made of dark stone and surrounded by a moat of swirling shadows. The fortress exuded a powerful, malevolent energy, and Seraphina could sense that the Shadow Core was inside.

As they approached the entrance, they were met by a horde of shadow creatures, their forms shifting and writhing as they advanced. Seraphina and Thorne prepared for battle, their magic crackling in the air.

The battle was fierce and relentless, the shadow creatures attacking with a ferocity that tested their skills and their bond. But Seraphina and Thorne fought with unwavering determination, their combined magic a force to be reckoned with.

With each defeated creature, they moved closer to the entrance of the fortress. Finally, after what felt like an eternity, they reached the massive doors, their bodies weary but their spirits unbroken.

"This is it," Seraphina said, her voice filled with resolve. "The Shadow Core is inside."

Thorne nodded, his eyes burning with determination. "Let's finish this."

They pushed open the doors and stepped into the fortress, the air thick with dark energy. The interior was vast and foreboding, with twisting corridors and towering columns that seemed to stretch on forever.

Guided by the light of the Celestial Amulet, they made their way through the fortress, their senses on high alert. As they ventured deeper, they could feel the presence of the sorcerer growing stronger, his malevolent energy pressing down on them like a suffocating weight.

Finally, they reached a grand chamber at the heart of the fortress. At the center of the chamber stood the Shadow Core, a massive, dark crystal that pulsed with a malevolent light. The sorcerer's spirit loomed over the crystal, his form twisted and malevolent.

"You dare to challenge me?" the sorcerer hissed, his voice filled with venom. "You will find that the power of the Shadow Core is beyond your comprehension."

Seraphina met the sorcerer's gaze with unwavering resolve. "We will break the curse and fulfill the prophecy. Your reign of terror ends today."

A battle of wills ensued, the air crackling with magical energy as Seraphina and Thorne confronted the sorcerer. The sorcerer's power was formidable, but Seraphina and Thorne's bond and determination proved to be a match for him.

With a final surge of energy, they directed their combined magic at the Shadow Core, the Celestial Amulet's light intensifying as it channeled their power. The dark crystal began to crack and shatter, its malevolent energy dissipating into the air.

The sorcerer let out a furious scream as his spirit was banished, his form dissolving into the shadows. The chamber was filled with a brilliant light as the Shadow Core was destroyed, and the oppressive energy lifted.

Seraphina and Thorne stood together, their bond stronger than ever. The curse that had bound them was broken, and the path to their future was clear.

With the Shadow Core destroyed and the sorcerer's spirit banished, Seraphina and Thorne made their way back to the portal that had brought them to the Shadow Realm. The journey was long and arduous, but the weight of the curse had been lifted, and their spirits were buoyed by the knowledge that they had fulfilled their destiny.

As they approached the portal, they were met once more by the guardian, its form shifting and ethereal. "You have succeeded where many have failed," the guardian said, its voice filled with approval. "The curse is broken, and the prophecy has been set in motion."

Seraphina nodded, her heart filled with gratitude. "Thank you for your guidance. We couldn't have done it without you."

The guardian's form shimmered with a soft light. "Your bond is your greatest strength. Trust in each other and in the light of the Celestial Amulet. The path ahead is still filled with challenges, but together, you can overcome anything."

With the guardian's blessing, Seraphina and Thorne stepped through the portal, leaving the Shadow Realm behind and returning to the familiar world of Eldergrove.

Back at the manor, the coven awaited their return, their faces filled with a mixture of anticipation and relief. High Priestess Elowen stepped forward, her eyes searching Seraphina's for answers.

"Seraphina, Thorne," Elowen said, her voice calm but filled with curiosity, "have you succeeded in your quest?"

Seraphina nodded, her heart lightened by their success. "Yes, High Priestess. We have destroyed the Shadow Core and broken the curse. The prophecy has been set in motion."

A murmur of approval and relief swept through the coven, and Elowen's eyes softened with pride. "You have proven yourselves once more. Your determination and strength have guided you through the trials, and you have succeeded where many would have failed."

Seraphina felt a surge of gratitude and pride. "Thank you, High Priestess. I could not have done it without the support of the coven and the bond I share with Thorne."

Elowen nodded, her gaze filled with wisdom. "The bond you share is a testament to the power of unity and determination. It is a reminder that even in the face of darkness and uncertainty, the strength of our connections can guide us through."

With the coven's approval and support, Seraphina and Thorne knew that their journey was just beginning. The challenges they had faced had strengthened their bond and prepared them for the trials ahead. Together, they would continue to uncover the secrets of the past, protect their legacy, and forge a new future.

As they looked toward the horizon, their hearts filled with hope and determination, they knew that the path before them was filled with challenges and opportunities. But with their bond and the power of the grimoire, they were ready to face whatever lay ahead. Their journey was far from over, and with each other by their side, there was nothing they could not achieve.

The Shadow Realm had tested their resolve and strengthened their bond, and they emerged stronger and more united than ever. As they looked toward the future, they knew that their journey was just beginning, and with each other by their side, there was nothing they could not achieve. Their bond was unbreakable, their determination unwavering, and their love for each other and their bloodlines a powerful force that would guide them through the darkest of times.

Chapter 8: The Phantom's Vengeance

The days following their return from the Shadow Realm were filled with a sense of accomplishment and purpose for Seraphina and Thorne. The prophecy had been set in motion, the curse broken, and the path to their future clearer than ever. Yet, despite their recent triumphs, a sense of unease lingered in the air. Thorne could feel it, a dark presence that seemed to shadow his every step, a reminder that his past was not entirely behind him.

One evening, as they sat by the fire in the study, Seraphina noticed Thorne's troubled expression. She reached out, placing a comforting hand on his arm. "Thorne, what's bothering you?"

Thorne sighed, his eyes reflecting the flickering flames. "I can't shake the feeling that something is coming. My past... it's not finished with me yet."

Seraphina's brow furrowed with concern. "What do you mean?"

Thorne looked at her, his gaze filled with a mixture of determination and vulnerability. "There are enemies from my past, powerful sorcerers who seek revenge. They know I've broken the curse, and they won't stop until they've destroyed me... and anyone who stands with me."

Seraphina's heart tightened with a mixture of fear and resolve. "Then we'll face them together. Whatever comes, we will stand strong."

Thorne nodded, his expression softening with gratitude. "Thank you, Seraphina. Your strength gives me hope."

Their conversation was interrupted by a sudden, chilling wind that swept through the room, extinguishing the fire and plunging the study into darkness. The air crackled with dark energy, and a sinister presence filled the room.

"They're here," Thorne said, his voice low and urgent.

In an instant, the room was filled with shadowy figures, their forms shifting and malevolent. Thorne and Seraphina stood back-to-back, their magic crackling in the air as they prepared for battle.

One of the figures stepped forward, its eyes glowing with a malevolent light. "Thorne Blackthorne," it hissed, "you thought you could escape your past, but you were wrong. We have come to exact our vengeance."

Thorne's eyes burned with determination. "I will not let you harm Seraphina or anyone else. This ends now."

The figure laughed, a cold, hollow sound. "We shall see."

With a flick of his wrist, Thorne unleashed a powerful blast of energy, sending the figure sprawling. The other shadows lunged towards them, their forms twisting and writhing as they attacked. Thorne and Seraphina fought with unwavering resolve, their magic a beacon of light in the darkness.

As the battle raged on, Thorne's powers were on full display. His magic was fierce and formidable, each spell a testament to his strength and skill. But despite his power, it was clear that he was also vulnerable. The years of being a phantom, the lingering effects of the curse, and the emotional toll of his past weighed heavily on him.

Seraphina could see the strain in his eyes, the weariness that threatened to overwhelm him. She knew she had to act, to protect him and ensure their victory. Summoning all her strength, she cast a protective barrier around them, the shimmering light repelling the shadows.

"Stay close to me," Seraphina said, her voice filled with determination.

Thorne nodded, his gratitude evident. "Thank you, Seraphina. Your magic is incredible."

As they fought side by side, Seraphina's magic proved pivotal. Her spells were precise and powerful, each one designed to protect and support Thorne. She drew on the strength of their bond, channeling her love and determination into every incantation.

Despite their combined efforts, the shadows continued to press forward, their malevolent energy growing stronger. Thorne could feel his strength waning, the weight of the battle taking its toll.

"Seraphina, I can't hold them off much longer," Thorne said, his voice strained.

Seraphina's heart pounded with fear and determination. "We have to find a way to end this. There must be something we can do."

In that moment, Seraphina remembered the Celestial Amulet, its light a powerful force against the darkness. She reached for the amulet, its warmth and energy filling her with renewed strength.

"Thorne, the amulet," she said urgently. "We can use its power to banish the shadows."

Thorne nodded, his eyes filled with hope. "Let's do it."

Together, they channeled their combined magic into the amulet, the air around them crackling with energy. The amulet's light intensified, casting a brilliant glow that pierced through the darkness.

With a final surge of power, they unleashed the amulet's energy, the light spreading out in a radiant wave that engulfed the shadows. The malevolent figures hissed and recoiled, their forms dissolving into the air.

As the last of the shadows vanished, the room was filled with a sense of calm and light. Seraphina and Thorne stood together, their bond stronger than ever.

"We did it," Seraphina said, her voice filled with relief.

Thorne nodded, his eyes filled with gratitude and admiration. "Thank you, Seraphina. I couldn't have done it without you."

Seraphina smiled, her heart filled with love. "We did it together, Thorne. Our bond is our greatest strength."

In the aftermath of the battle, Seraphina and Thorne took a moment to catch their breath and assess the situation. The study was in disarray, the remnants of the dark energy lingering in the air.

"We need to find out who sent those shadows," Thorne said, his voice filled with determination. "They won't stop until they've destroyed us."

Seraphina nodded, her resolve firm. "We'll find them, Thorne. And we'll stop them. Together."

As they began to investigate, they discovered a series of ancient symbols and runes etched into the floor where the shadows had appeared. The symbols were unfamiliar, but their dark energy was unmistakable.

"We need to decipher these symbols," Seraphina said, her brow furrowed with concentration. "They might give us a clue about who we're dealing with."

Thorne nodded, his expression serious. "I'll start researching in the grimoire. There must be something in there that can help us."

As they worked together, their determination and bond guided their efforts. The symbols were complex and cryptic, but Seraphina's sharp mind and Thorne's extensive knowledge of magic proved invaluable.

After hours of intense study, they finally uncovered the meaning behind the symbols. They were a mark of a powerful sorcerer from Thorne's past, a mage named Kaelith who had once been an ally but had turned against him in a bid for power.

"Kaelith," Thorne said, his voice filled with a mixture of anger and resolve. "He was one of the most ambitious and ruthless sorcerers I've ever known. He'll stop at nothing to destroy us."

Seraphina's eyes burned with determination. "Then we need to stop him first. We'll find Kaelith and put an end to his plans."

With their path clear, Seraphina and Thorne began to prepare for their next journey. The battle with the shadows had revealed the full extent of their powers and vulnerabilities, and they knew that facing Kaelith would be their greatest challenge yet.

As they gathered their supplies and prepared their spells, they took a moment to reflect on their journey so far. The trials they had faced had strengthened their bond and their resolve, and they were more determined than ever to protect each other and fulfill their destiny.

"Thorne," Seraphina said, her voice filled with love and determination, "whatever happens, we'll face it together. Our bond is our greatest strength, and we'll use it to overcome any challenge."

Thorne nodded, his eyes filled with gratitude and hope. "Together, we can overcome anything. I believe in us, Seraphina."

With their hearts and minds united, Seraphina and Thorne set off on their journey to find Kaelith and put an end to his plans. The path ahead was filled with danger and uncertainty, but their bond and determination would guide them through the darkest of times.

The journey to find Kaelith led them to a remote and treacherous region known as the Darkspire Mountains. The landscape was harsh and unforgiving, with jagged peaks and deep ravines that tested their endurance and resolve.

As they ventured deeper into the mountains, they could feel the dark energy of Kaelith's presence growing stronger. The air was thick with malevolent magic, and the shadows seemed to whisper and shift around them.

"We must be getting close," Seraphina said, her voice filled with determination. "Kaelith's energy is everywhere."

Thorne nodded, his expression serious. "Stay alert. He'll have traps and defenses set up to protect himself."

Their journey led them to a massive, ancient fortress built into the side of a mountain. The fortress exuded a powerful, malevolent energy, and Seraphina could sense that Kaelith was inside.

As they approached the entrance, they were met by a series of powerful magical barriers and traps. Seraphina and Thorne worked together, their combined magic a force to be reckoned with. They dismantled the traps and broke through the barriers, their bond and determination guiding their every move.

Inside the fortress, the air was thick with dark energy, and the interior was a labyrinth of twisting corridors and hidden chambers. Guided by the Celestial Amulet, they navigated the maze-like structure, their senses on high alert.

Finally, they reached the heart of the fortress, where Kaelith awaited them. The sorcerer stood at the center of a grand chamber, his eyes burning with a malevolent light.

"Thorne," Kaelith sneered, his voice filled with venom. "I knew you would come. But you are too late. The power of the Shadow Core will be mine, and I will destroy you both."

Thorne's eyes burned with determination. "We will stop you, Kaelith. Your reign of terror ends today."

A battle of epic proportions ensued, the air crackling with magical energy as Thorne and Seraphina confronted Kaelith. The sorcerer's power was formidable, but Thorne and Seraphina's bond and determination proved to be a match for him.

Seraphina's magic was pivotal in the battle. Her spells were precise and powerful, each one designed to protect and support Thorne. She drew on the strength of their bond, channeling her love and determination into every incantation.

Despite their combined efforts, Kaelith's power was overwhelming. Thorne could feel his strength waning, the weight of the battle taking its toll.

"Seraphina, I can't hold him off much longer," Thorne said, his voice strained.

Seraphina's heart pounded with fear and determination. "We have to find a way to end this. There must be something we can do."

In that moment, Seraphina remembered the Celestial Amulet, its light a powerful force against the darkness. She reached for the amulet, its warmth and energy filling her with renewed strength.

"Thorne, the amulet," she said urgently. "We can use its power to defeat Kaelith."

Thorne nodded, his eyes filled with hope. "Let's do it."

Together, they channeled their combined magic into the amulet, the air around them crackling with energy. The amulet's light intensified, casting a brilliant glow that pierced through the darkness.

With a final surge of power, they unleashed the amulet's energy, the light spreading out in a radiant wave that engulfed Kaelith. The sorcerer screamed in fury as his power was shattered, his form dissolving into the air.

As the last of Kaelith's energy dissipated, the chamber was filled with a sense of calm and light. Seraphina and Thorne stood together, their bond stronger than ever.

"We did it," Seraphina said, her voice filled with relief.

Thorne nodded, his eyes filled with gratitude and admiration. "Thank you, Seraphina. I couldn't have done it without you."

Seraphina smiled, her heart filled with love. "We did it together, Thorne. Our bond is our greatest strength."

In the aftermath of the battle, Seraphina and Thorne took a moment to catch their breath and reflect on their journey. The trials they had faced had strengthened their bond and their resolve, and they were more determined than ever to protect each other and fulfill their destiny.

As they made their way back to the Nightshade manor, they knew that their journey was far from over. The dark forces that had threatened them were still out there, and new challenges awaited them. But with their bond and the power of the Celestial Amulet, they were ready to face whatever lay ahead.

Back at the manor, the coven awaited their return, their faces filled with a mixture of anticipation and relief. High Priestess Elowen stepped forward, her eyes searching Seraphina's for answers.

"Seraphina, Thorne," Elowen said, her voice calm but filled with curiosity, "have you succeeded in your quest?"

Seraphina nodded, her heart lightened by their success. "Yes, High Priestess. We have defeated Kaelith and ended his threat. The path to our future is clear."

A murmur of approval and relief swept through the coven, and Elowen's eyes softened with pride. "You have proven yourselves once more. Your determination and strength have guided you through the trials, and you have succeeded where many would have failed."

Seraphina felt a surge of gratitude and pride. "Thank you, High Priestess. I could not have done it without the support of the coven and the bond I share with Thorne."

Elowen nodded, her gaze filled with wisdom. "The bond you share is a testament to the power of unity and determination. It is a reminder that even in the face of darkness and uncertainty, the strength of our connections can guide us through."

With the coven's approval and support, Seraphina and Thorne knew that their journey was just beginning. The challenges they had faced had strengthened their bond and prepared them for the trials ahead. Together, they would continue to uncover the secrets of the past, protect their legacy, and forge a new future.

As they looked toward the horizon, their hearts filled with hope and determination, they knew that the path before them was filled with challenges and opportunities. But with their bond and the power of the grimoire, they were ready to face whatever lay ahead. Their journey was far from over, and with each other by their side, there was nothing they could not achieve.

The battle with Kaelith had tested their resolve and strengthened their bond, and they emerged stronger and more united than ever. As they looked toward the future, they knew that their journey was just beginning, and with each other by their side, there was nothing they could not achieve. Their bond was unbreakable, their determination unwavering, and their love for each other and their bloodlines a powerful force that would guide them through the darkest of times.

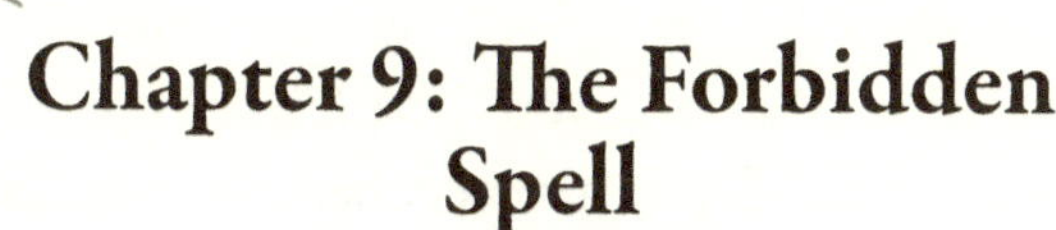

Chapter 9: The Forbidden Spell

The early morning light filtered through the stained-glass windows of the Nightshade manor, casting a kaleidoscope of colors on the stone floor. Seraphina sat at the heavy oak table in the study, the ancient grimoire open before her. The book had revealed many secrets, but the one she had discovered last night left her both hopeful and terrified.

Seraphina traced her fingers over the delicate, faded script of the grimoire's newest revelation—a forbidden spell that promised to break Thorne's curse. The spell was powerful and ancient, known as the Spell of Eternal Release. However, its potential came with a dire warning: the spell required a significant sacrifice from the caster.

Her thoughts were interrupted as Thorne entered the study, his presence filling the room with a comforting warmth. He had become her confidant, her partner in magic, and her closest friend. She couldn't imagine her life without him.

"Good morning," Thorne greeted, his voice calm and steady. "You look troubled."

Seraphina sighed, her eyes meeting his. "I found something in the grimoire. It's a spell that could break your curse, but it's a forbidden spell. The Spell of Eternal Release."

Thorne's eyes widened with a mixture of hope and apprehension. "What does it require?"

Seraphina took a deep breath, her voice wavering. "It requires a significant sacrifice from the caster. The spell demands a part of their life force, something that could leave the caster weakened or... worse."

The weight of her words hung in the air, and Thorne's expression darkened. "Seraphina, I can't let you risk your life for me."

Seraphina's eyes filled with determination. "Thorne, I'm willing to do whatever it takes to free you from this curse. You've suffered for centuries, and if there's a chance I can help you, I have to try."

Thorne shook his head, his voice filled with emotion. "But the risks are too great. What if something happens to you? I couldn't bear it."

Seraphina reached out and took his hand, her grip firm. "Thorne, you mean the world to me. I can't stand by and do nothing when I know there's a way to help you. Please, let me try."

Thorne's eyes met hers, filled with gratitude and conflict. He knew how much this meant to her, but the thought of losing her was unbearable. "Seraphina, I trust you with my life. But please, promise me you'll be careful."

Seraphina nodded, her resolve unwavering. "I promise, Thorne. We'll do this together."

The next few days were a whirlwind of preparation. Seraphina and Thorne studied the grimoire meticulously, ensuring they understood every aspect of the Spell of Eternal Release. The spell required rare ingredients and precise incantations, and they couldn't afford any mistakes.

As they gathered the necessary components, the weight of the impending ritual pressed down on Seraphina. She couldn't help but feel the tension between her desire to help Thorne and the risks involved. The thought of the sacrifice loomed over her, a constant reminder of what was at stake.

One evening, as they sat by the fire, Seraphina voiced her fears. "Thorne, what if something goes wrong? What if I'm not strong enough to perform the spell?"

Thorne's eyes softened with compassion. "Seraphina, you are one of the strongest people I know. We've faced countless challenges together, and we've always come through. Trust in yourself, and trust in our bond."

Seraphina leaned into his reassuring presence, drawing strength from his words. "Thank you, Thorne. I'll do my best."

The night before the ritual, Seraphina found herself unable to sleep. She wandered the halls of the manor, her mind racing with thoughts of the spell and its consequences. As she passed by the grand hall, she paused before the portraits of her ancestors. Their faces seemed to watch her, a silent reminder of the legacy she carried.

She whispered a prayer to them, asking for their guidance and strength. "Please, help me find the courage to do what needs to be done."

The day of the ritual arrived, and the manor was filled with an air of anticipation and tension. Seraphina and Thorne had prepared the ritual chamber, a room deep within the manor that was lined with protective wards and enchantments.

The ingredients were arranged meticulously, and the grimoire lay open on a pedestal at the center of the room. The Celestial Amulet hung around Seraphina's neck, its light a beacon of hope.

As they stood before the pedestal, Seraphina took Thorne's hand, her voice steady. "Are you ready?"

Thorne nodded, his eyes filled with determination. "Yes. Let's do this."

Seraphina began the incantation, her voice resonating with power. The air around them shimmered with a dark energy, and the ingredients began to glow with an ethereal light. Thorne joined her, their voices merging in perfect harmony.

As the incantation reached its climax, Seraphina felt a surge of energy coursing through her. The grimoire's pages seemed to come alive, the symbols glowing with an intense light. She could feel the spell drawing on her life force, the sacrifice demanded by the ritual.

The room was filled with a brilliant light as the spell took hold, the energy enveloping Thorne in a cocoon of magic. Seraphina's strength waned, but she held on, determined to see the spell through.

"Seraphina, hold on!" Thorne shouted, his voice filled with concern.

With a final burst of energy, the spell reached its peak, and the room was filled with a deafening silence. The light faded, and Seraphina collapsed to the floor, her strength completely spent.

Thorne rushed to her side, his heart pounding with fear. "Seraphina, are you alright?"

Seraphina's eyes fluttered open, her voice weak. "Thorne... did it work?"

Thorne's eyes filled with tears of relief and gratitude. "Yes, Seraphina. The curse is broken. You did it."

Seraphina smiled, her heart filled with joy despite her exhaustion. "I'm so glad... you're free."

As Thorne helped her to her feet, they embraced, their bond stronger than ever. They had faced the ultimate test of their commitment and bravery, and they had succeeded.

THE DAYS FOLLOWING the ritual were a time of healing and reflection for Seraphina and Thorne. The effects of the spell had left Seraphina weakened, but with Thorne's support and the coven's care, she began to regain her strength.

The coven was overjoyed at their success, and High Priestess Elowen praised Seraphina's bravery and dedication. "You have shown incredible strength, Seraphina. Your actions have not only freed Thorne but have also strengthened the bond of our coven."

Seraphina felt a deep sense of gratitude and pride. "Thank you, High Priestess. I couldn't have done it without Thorne and the support of the coven."

Elowen nodded, her eyes filled with wisdom. "The bond you share is a testament to the power of unity and love. It is a reminder that even in the face of great sacrifice, the strength of our connections can guide us through."

As Seraphina and Thorne continued to recover, they took the time to reflect on their journey and the challenges they had faced. The spell had tested their commitment and bravery, but it had also deepened their bond and their resolve to protect each other and the magical world.

One evening, as they sat by the fire, Thorne took Seraphina's hand, his eyes filled with love. "Seraphina, you have given me the greatest gift I could ever ask for. You freed me from a curse that had bound me for centuries. I can never repay you for what you've done."

Seraphina smiled, her heart filled with warmth. "You don't need to repay me, Thorne. Your presence in my life is enough. Together, we can face whatever challenges come our way."

Thorne nodded, his eyes reflecting the flickering flames. "Together, we are stronger. Our bond is our greatest strength."

As they looked toward the future, their hearts filled with hope and determination, they knew that their journey was far from over. The forbidden spell had revealed the depth of their love and commitment, and they were ready to face whatever challenges lay ahead.

In the weeks that followed, Seraphina and Thorne continued to study the grimoire, uncovering more secrets and preparing for the trials that awaited them. The spell had left a lasting impact on Seraphina, but with each passing day, she grew stronger and more determined.

Their bond had been tested and proven unbreakable, and they were more united than ever in their quest to protect the magical world. The coven, inspired by their bravery and dedication, rallied around them, offering their support and guidance.

One evening, as they studied a particularly complex passage in the grimoire, Seraphina felt a sudden surge of energy. The pages seemed to come alive, revealing a new section of text that had been hidden until now.

"Thorne, look at this," Seraphina said, her voice filled with excitement. "The grimoire is revealing more about the prophecy."

Thorne leaned in, his eyes scanning the newly revealed text. "It speaks of a powerful artifact, the Heart of Eternity. It is said to hold the key to unlocking the full potential of the prophecy and protecting the magical world from the forces of darkness."

Seraphina's heart raced with excitement. "We need to find this artifact. It could be the key to fulfilling our destiny."

Thorne nodded, his expression serious. "But the artifact is likely well-guarded. We must be prepared for whatever challenges lie ahead."

With their path clear, Seraphina and Thorne began to prepare for their next journey. The challenges they had faced had strengthened their bond and their resolve, and they were more determined than ever to protect each other and fulfill their destiny.

As they gathered their supplies and prepared their spells, they took a moment to reflect on their journey so far. The trials they had faced had tested their commitment and bravery, but they had emerged stronger and more united than ever.

"Thorne," Seraphina said, her voice filled with love and determination, "whatever happens, we'll face it together. Our bond is our greatest strength, and we'll use it to overcome any challenge."

Thorne nodded, his eyes filled with gratitude and hope. "Together, we can overcome anything. I believe in us, Seraphina."

With their hearts and minds united, Seraphina and Thorne set off on their journey to find the Heart of Eternity and unlock the full potential of the prophecy. The path ahead was filled with danger and uncertainty, but their bond and determination would guide them through the darkest of times.

As they looked toward the horizon, their hearts filled with hope and determination, they knew that their journey was just beginning. The forbidden spell had revealed the depth of their love and commitment, and with each other by their side, there was nothing they could not achieve.

Their bond was unbreakable, their determination unwavering, and their love for each other and their bloodlines a powerful force that would guide them through the darkest of times.

Chapter 10: The Phantom Hunter

The tranquility of Eldergrove was shattered with the arrival of a stranger. Tall and cloaked in dark leather, he exuded an aura of menace and determination. His presence did not go unnoticed; villagers whispered of his cold, calculating demeanor and the arsenal of weapons he carried. The stranger was a phantom hunter, known only as Lucien, and his arrival heralded a storm that would test Seraphina and Thorne like never before.

Lucien's reputation preceded him. He was infamous for his relentless pursuit of phantoms, driven by a vendetta that had consumed him for years. His eyes, cold and unyielding, seemed to pierce through anyone who dared to meet his gaze. He carried an arsenal of enchanted weapons, each designed to capture or destroy phantoms.

Seraphina and Thorne were in the study, poring over the grimoire, when they first heard the news. A knock on the door interrupted their work, and Seraphina's heart skipped a beat as she saw the anxious face of one of the coven's messengers.

"Seraphina, Thorne," the young witch said, her voice trembling. "There's a phantom hunter in the village. He's asking about Thorne."

Seraphina's eyes widened with alarm, and she turned to Thorne, who was already on his feet, his expression grim. "We need to go into hiding," he said, his voice filled with urgency. "We can't let him find us."

Seraphina nodded, her heart pounding with fear. "Let's gather what we need and leave immediately."

AS THEY HURRIEDLY PACKED their essentials, Seraphina's mind raced. The arrival of the phantom hunter was unexpected, and the danger was palpable. She couldn't help but wonder why Lucien had come to Eldergrove and what had driven him to hunt phantoms with such fervor.

"Thorne," she said as they made their way through the hidden passages of the manor, "do you know anything about this hunter? Why is he so determined to capture you?"

Thorne's expression was dark, his voice low and filled with bitterness. "Lucien has a personal vendetta against phantoms. His family was attacked by a rogue phantom when he was a child, and he watched helplessly as his parents were killed. Since then, he's dedicated his life to hunting down and destroying phantoms, believing that all of us are malevolent."

Seraphina's heart ached for Thorne and the pain of his past. "But you're not like that, Thorne. You're not a threat."

Thorne's eyes met hers, filled with a mixture of sorrow and determination. "Lucien doesn't see it that way. To him, I'm just another phantom to be hunted."

They reached a hidden chamber deep within the manor, a place where they could stay out of sight while they devised a plan. The chamber was dimly lit, and the air was filled with the scent of ancient herbs and protective enchantments.

"We need to figure out how to deal with Lucien," Seraphina said, her voice steady despite the fear gnawing at her. "We can't stay hidden forever."

Thorne nodded, his mind racing. "We need to find a way to convince him that I'm not a threat. But that's easier said than done. Lucien is relentless and won't stop until he's captured me."

Meanwhile, in the village, Lucien's presence was causing a stir. He interrogated villagers, his cold eyes searching for any sign of the phantom he sought. His methods were ruthless, his determination unwavering.

Lucien's background was a tragic one. Born into a family of skilled hunters, he had been trained in the art of tracking and combat from a young age. But his life had been forever altered when a rogue phantom attacked his family. Lucien had survived, but his parents had not. The trauma had fueled his obsession with hunting phantoms, and he had become one of the most feared hunters in the land.

Lucien's vendetta was not just against the phantom that had killed his parents, but against all phantoms. He believed that their very existence was a threat to humanity and that they needed to be eradicated. His encounters with malevolent phantoms had only solidified this belief, and he had become relentless in his pursuit.

As Lucien gathered information in the village, he began to piece together the clues that would lead him to Thorne. The villagers, fearful and uncertain, provided bits of information that hinted at Thorne's presence. Lucien's determination grew stronger with each passing moment.

In the hidden chamber, Seraphina and Thorne were deep in conversation, trying to devise a plan. "We need to find a way to communicate with Lucien," Seraphina said, her voice filled with determination. "If we can make him see reason, maybe we can avoid a confrontation."

Thorne nodded, his eyes filled with hope. "But how do we reach him without putting ourselves at risk? Lucien is dangerous, and he won't hesitate to use force."

Seraphina's mind raced, searching for a solution. "We need to find a way to show him that you're not a threat. Maybe if we can find proof of your innocence, something that demonstrates your true nature, we can convince him."

Thorne's eyes lit up with a glimmer of hope. "There's an old journal hidden in the manor, written by one of my ancestors. It details our family's history and the curse that was placed on us. If we can show that to Lucien, it might make him understand."

Seraphina's heart raced with excitement. "Let's find it. It might be our only chance."

As they searched the manor for the journal, the air was thick with tension. The hidden passages and chambers were filled with the echoes of their footsteps, and every shadow seemed to hold a hint of danger.

Finally, they found the journal, hidden in a dusty, forgotten corner of the manor's library. The leather-bound book was old and worn, its pages filled with the delicate script of Thorne's ancestors.

"This is it," Thorne said, his voice filled with a mixture of relief and determination. "We need to get this to Lucien."

Seraphina nodded, her heart pounding. "But how? We can't just walk up to him. It's too risky."

Thorne's mind raced, searching for a solution. "We need a mediator, someone who can approach Lucien without arousing suspicion. Someone he might trust."

Seraphina's eyes lit up with an idea. "What about High Priestess Elowen? She has the respect of the villagers and the knowledge of our magic. She might be able to convince Lucien to listen."

Thorne nodded, his expression serious. "It's worth a try. Let's go to her."

High Priestess Elowen listened intently as Seraphina and Thorne explained the situation. Her wise eyes were filled with concern and determination.

"Lucien is a formidable adversary," Elowen said, her voice calm but serious. "But I believe in the strength of our bond and the truth of your story. I will speak to him and try to make him see reason."

Seraphina and Thorne exchanged grateful glances. "Thank you, High Priestess. Your help means everything to us," Seraphina said.

Elowen nodded, her eyes filled with resolve. "Stay hidden and safe. I will do everything in my power to protect you."

Elowen approached Lucien in the village square, her presence commanding respect. The villagers watched with a mixture of curiosity and apprehension as she confronted the phantom hunter.

"Lucien," Elowen said, her voice steady and authoritative. "I am High Priestess Elowen of the Nightshade coven. I understand you are here to hunt a phantom, but I implore you to listen to reason."

Lucien's cold eyes narrowed as he regarded her. "Why should I listen to you, witch? My mission is clear. I will not rest until I have captured the phantom."

Elowen met his gaze, her voice unwavering. "The phantom you seek is Thorne Blackthorne, and he is not the malevolent being you believe him to be. He is a victim of a curse, bound by forces beyond his control. I have proof of his innocence."

Lucien's expression remained skeptical, but there was a hint of curiosity in his eyes. "Show me this proof."

Elowen produced the journal, its worn pages a testament to its age. "This journal belongs to Thorne's ancestors. It details the history of his family and the curse that was placed on them. Read it, and you will see the truth."

Lucien hesitated for a moment before taking the journal. His eyes scanned the pages, his expression slowly changing from skepticism to intrigue.

As he read, Elowen continued to speak. "Thorne has lived for centuries under the weight of this curse. He seeks only to find peace and redemption. He is not a threat to anyone."

Lucien's eyes flickered with a mixture of emotions as he closed the journal. "If what you say is true, then Thorne is indeed a victim. But how can I be sure this is not a trick?"

Elowen's gaze was steady. "I give you my word as High Priestess. Thorne is innocent. Please, give him a chance to explain himself."

Back in the hidden chamber, Seraphina and Thorne waited anxiously for Elowen's return. The tension was palpable, and every passing moment felt like an eternity.

Finally, they heard the sound of footsteps approaching. Elowen entered the chamber, her expression a mixture of relief and determination.

"Lucien has agreed to meet with you," Elowen said, her voice calm but serious. "He is willing to listen, but be cautious. He is still wary and could be dangerous."

Seraphina's heart raced with a mixture of hope and fear. "Thank you, High Priestess. We'll be careful."

Thorne nodded, his eyes filled with gratitude. "Thank you, Elowen. This might be our only chance."

The meeting with Lucien was arranged in a secluded glade on the outskirts of the village. Seraphina and Thorne approached cautiously, their hearts pounding with anticipation.

Lucien stood in the center of the glade, his expression guarded but curious. The journal was in his hand, a silent reminder of the truth it held.

"Thorne Blackthorne," Lucien said, his voice cold and steady. "High Priestess Elowen has spoken on your behalf. I am here to listen, but know that I will not hesitate to act if I sense any deception."

Thorne nodded, his expression serious. "I understand, Lucien. I have nothing to hide."

Seraphina stepped forward, her voice calm and steady. "Lucien, Thorne is not the monster you believe him to be. He is a victim of a curse, bound by forces beyond his control. He seeks only to find peace and redemption."

Lucien's eyes flickered with a mixture of emotions. "I have read the journal. It speaks of a curse, but how can I be sure it is true? How can I trust a phantom?"

Thorne's eyes met Lucien's, filled with a mixture of sorrow and determination. "I understand your pain, Lucien. I have lived for centuries under the weight of this curse, seeking redemption for the sins of my ancestors. I have never harmed anyone, and I only seek to find peace."

Lucien's expression remained guarded, but there was a hint of doubt in his eyes. "Why should I believe you? My family was killed by a phantom. How can I trust that you are different?"

Thorne's voice was filled with emotion. "Because I know what it means to lose everything. I have lived with the pain of my past, seeking a way to make amends. I am not your enemy, Lucien. I am just a soul seeking redemption."

Lucien's eyes softened, his expression conflicted. "If what you say is true, then I have been wrong in my quest. I have hunted phantoms without understanding their true nature."

Seraphina's voice was gentle but firm. "Lucien, you have the power to make a difference. To stop the cycle of vengeance and seek understanding instead. Thorne is not a threat. He is a victim, just like you."

Lucien's gaze met hers, and for the first time, there was a glimmer of hope in his eyes. "Perhaps... perhaps you are right. I have spent my life driven by hatred and revenge. It is time to seek a different path."

The tension in the glade began to dissipate, replaced by a sense of understanding and hope. Lucien's vendetta against phantoms had been born of pain and loss, but now, faced with the truth, he began to see the possibility of redemption.

"Thorne," Lucien said, his voice filled with a mixture of apology and determination, "I will cease my hunt. You have shown me that not all phantoms are malevolent. Perhaps it is time for me to find a new purpose."

Thorne's eyes filled with gratitude. "Thank you, Lucien. Your understanding means more to me than you know."

Seraphina's heart swelled with relief and hope. "Thank you, Lucien. This is a new beginning for all of us."

In the days that followed, Lucien remained in Eldergrove, seeking to understand more about the magical world and the true nature of phantoms. He spent time with the coven, learning about their ways and seeking redemption for his past actions.

Seraphina and Thorne continued their quest, their bond stronger than ever. The encounter with Lucien had tested their resolve and commitment, but it had also opened a new path of understanding and hope.

One evening, as they sat by the fire in the study, Seraphina turned to Thorne, her voice filled with love and determination. "Thorne, we have faced so many challenges together, and we have always come through. I believe in our bond, and I believe in us."

Thorne's eyes met hers, filled with gratitude and hope. "Together, we can overcome anything. Our bond is our greatest strength."

As they looked toward the future, their hearts filled with hope and determination, they knew that their journey was far from over. The challenges they had faced had tested their commitment and bravery, but they had emerged stronger and more united than ever.

Their bond was unbreakable, their determination unwavering, and their love for each other and their bloodlines a powerful force that would guide them through the darkest of times. The encounter with the phantom hunter had revealed the depth of their strength and commitment, and with each other by their side, there was nothing they could not achieve.

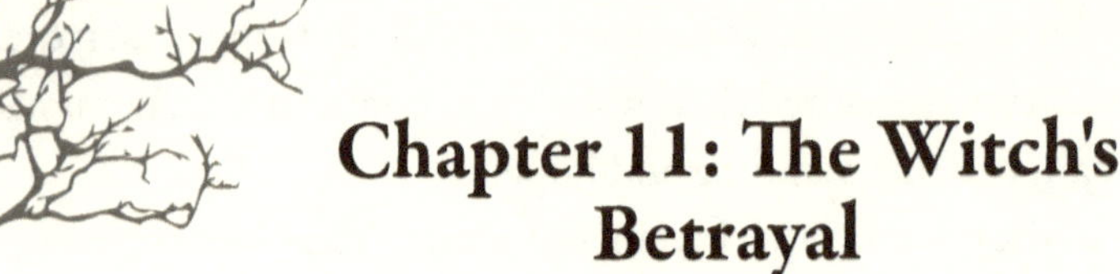

Chapter 11: The Witch's Betrayal

The serene atmosphere of Eldergrove was an illusion. Beneath its tranquil surface, tensions simmered. The recent events had brought Seraphina and Thorne closer than ever, but not all within the coven shared their bond or their vision. The peace they had fought so hard to maintain was about to be shattered from within.

The morning dawned with an ominous stillness. Seraphina awoke with a sense of unease that she couldn't shake. She dressed quickly and made her way to the study, where Thorne was already pouring over the grimoire. The light from the window cast a warm glow over the room, but the heaviness in the air belied the beautiful day outside.

"Good morning," Seraphina greeted, trying to mask her anxiety.

Thorne looked up, his eyes filled with concern. "Morning. You look troubled."

"I just have a feeling," she admitted. "Something isn't right."

Before Thorne could respond, the door to the study burst open, and one of the younger coven members, Marla, rushed in, her face pale with fear.

"Seraphina, Thorne, you need to come to the council chamber immediately. There's been... an incident."

Seraphina's heart sank. "What happened?"

"It's Elowen. She's been accused of betraying the coven."

The council chamber was filled with tension. Covens from neighboring villages had gathered, their expressions a mixture of anger and disbelief. High Priestess Elowen stood at the center, her normally calm and composed demeanor replaced by a look of shock and betrayal.

Seraphina and Thorne pushed through the crowd, their presence immediately noticed by all. Seraphina's eyes met Elowen's, seeking understanding.

"What is going on here?" Seraphina demanded, her voice steady but filled with authority.

A senior coven member, Talia, stepped forward. "Seraphina, it has come to our attention that Elowen has been communicating with outside forces. Forces that seek to expose Thorne and disrupt our plans."

Elowen shook her head, her voice trembling. "This is not true! I have done no such thing."

Talia continued, ignoring Elowen's protest. "We have found evidence. Correspondence with known phantom hunters and other factions who oppose our ways."

The room erupted in murmurs and accusations. Seraphina felt a wave of dizziness. High Priestess Elowen, who had guided and supported her through every trial, accused of betrayal? It seemed unthinkable.

Thorne's voice cut through the chaos. "Let us see this evidence."

Talia handed over a bundle of letters, each one bearing Elowen's seal. Seraphina's heart pounded as she read through the contents. The letters detailed plans and information about Thorne and the coven's activities, written in a style that closely resembled Elowen's hand.

Elowen's eyes were filled with desperation. "Those are forgeries! I swear it. Someone is trying to frame me."

Seraphina felt the weight of the decision pressing down on her. She had to trust her instincts and her bond with Elowen, but the evidence was damning.

"Everyone, listen!" Seraphina's voice rang out, commanding attention. "We cannot make any hasty decisions. We need to investigate further before we condemn anyone."

The coven members exchanged uncertain glances, but Seraphina's authority was unquestionable. Reluctantly, they agreed to hold off on any action until a thorough investigation could be conducted.

The next few days were a whirlwind of investigation and suspicion. Seraphina and Thorne worked tirelessly, scrutinizing every detail of the letters and questioning members of the coven. The atmosphere in the manor was tense, with trust in short supply.

Seraphina spent hours with Elowen, trying to uncover any clue that could prove her innocence. Elowen was devastated by the accusations, but her resolve remained strong.

"Seraphina," Elowen said one evening, her voice weary but determined, "you must believe me. I have done nothing to betray the coven. There is a deeper plot here, and we must find out who is truly behind it."

Seraphina squeezed Elowen's hand. "I believe you. We will find the truth."

As they delved deeper into the investigation, they discovered discrepancies in the letters—subtle differences in the handwriting and phrasing that suggested forgery. Seraphina's suspicion grew, but she needed more concrete evidence.

Thorne suggested searching the council chamber for any clues that might have been overlooked. Late one night, they snuck into the chamber, their hearts pounding with anticipation.

Hidden beneath a loose floorboard, they found a stash of documents and correspondence that linked Talia to outside factions. The evidence was clear: Talia had orchestrated the betrayal, forging the letters to frame Elowen and sow discord within the coven.

"We have to confront her," Seraphina said, her voice filled with determination.

The next day, Seraphina called a meeting of the entire coven. The atmosphere was charged with tension as everyone gathered in the council chamber. Talia stood confidently, but there was a flicker of uncertainty in her eyes.

"Thank you all for coming," Seraphina began, her voice steady. "We have conducted a thorough investigation into the accusations against High Priestess Elowen. What we have uncovered is shocking."

She revealed the forged letters and the hidden documents, laying out the evidence for all to see. "These documents prove that Talia has been working with outside forces to frame Elowen and disrupt our coven. This betrayal runs deep, and we must address it."

The room erupted in shocked gasps and angry murmurs. Talia's confident facade crumbled as she realized the extent of her exposure.

"You cannot believe this!" Talia shouted, her voice filled with desperation. "I did what I thought was necessary to protect the coven!"

Elowen stepped forward, her voice calm but resolute. "Protecting the coven does not mean betraying your sisters and brothers. You have sown discord and mistrust, and for that, you must be held accountable."

The coven members, their anger and betrayal palpable, demanded justice. Talia was stripped of her rank and exiled from the coven, her actions condemned by all.

In the aftermath of the betrayal, the coven was left to pick up the pieces. The split was deep, with some members still reeling from the shock of the betrayal and others rallying behind Seraphina and Elowen.

High Priestess Elowen addressed the coven, her voice filled with determination. "We have faced a great trial, but we are stronger for it. We must rebuild our trust and unity, and continue our work to protect the magical world."

Seraphina stood by Elowen's side, her resolve unwavering. "We will overcome this. Our bond is our greatest strength, and we will not let this betrayal tear us apart."

Thorne, ever supportive, added, "We have faced many challenges together, and we have always come through. This will be no different."

As the days turned into weeks, the coven began to heal. Seraphina and Thorne continued their work, uncovering more secrets of the grimoire and preparing for the trials that lay ahead. The betrayal had tested their resolve and commitment, but it had also strengthened their bond and their determination to protect each other and their coven.

One evening, as they sat by the fire in the study, Seraphina turned to Thorne, her voice filled with love and determination. "Thorne, we have faced so many challenges together, and we have always come through. I believe in our bond, and I believe in us."

Thorne's eyes met hers, filled with gratitude and hope. "Together, we can overcome anything. Our bond is our greatest strength."

As they looked toward the future, their hearts filled with hope and determination, they knew that their journey was far from over. The betrayal had revealed the depth of their strength and commitment, and with each other by their side, there was nothing they could not achieve.

Their bond was unbreakable, their determination unwavering, and their love for each other and their bloodlines a powerful force that would guide them through the darkest of times. The betrayal within the coven had tested their resolve, but it had also shown them the true strength of their unity and their love.

As the coven continued to rebuild, Seraphina and Thorne focused on their next steps. The grimoire had revealed much, but there were still many secrets to uncover and challenges to face. Their journey was far from over, and they were ready to face whatever lay ahead.

"Seraphina," Thorne said one evening, his voice filled with determination, "we have come so far, but there is still much to do. The prophecy is still unfolding, and we must be prepared for whatever comes next."

Seraphina nodded, her resolve firm. "I know, Thorne. And we will face it together. Our bond and our love will guide us through."

With their hearts and minds united, Seraphina and Thorne set off on their next journey, their bond stronger than ever. The betrayal within the coven had tested them, but it had also shown them the true strength of their love and their unity.

As they looked toward the horizon, their hearts filled with hope and determination, they knew that their journey was just beginning. The challenges they had faced had tested their commitment and bravery, but they had emerged stronger and more united than ever.

Their bond was unbreakable, their determination unwavering, and their love for each other and their bloodlines a powerful force that would guide

them through the darkest of times. The betrayal within the coven had revealed the depth of their strength and commitment, and with each other by their side, there was nothing they could not achieve.

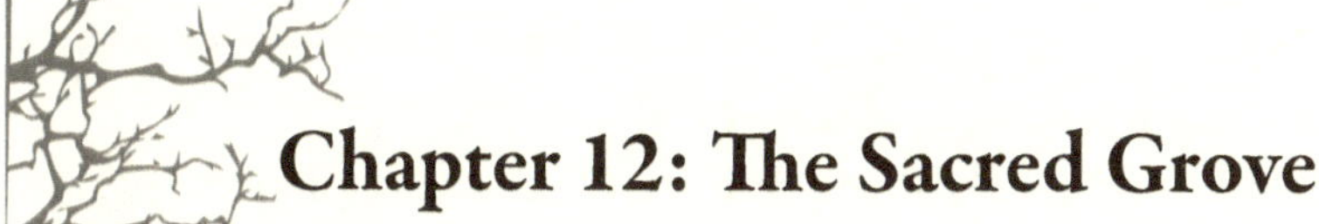

Chapter 12: The Sacred Grove

The aftermath of the betrayal within the coven had left Seraphina and Thorne both exhausted and wary. Trust was a fragile thing, easily shattered, and they needed a place of sanctuary to gather their strength and plan their next move. High Priestess Elowen suggested they seek refuge in the Sacred Grove, an ancient place known for its powerful protective magic.

The journey to the Sacred Grove took them deep into the heart of the forest, where the trees were tall and ancient, their branches weaving a dense canopy that filtered the sunlight into a soft, green glow. The air was filled with the scent of pine and earth, and the sounds of birds and rustling leaves created a serene symphony.

Seraphina and Thorne traveled in silence, the weight of recent events heavy on their minds. They had faced betrayal, uncovered plots, and strengthened their bond, but they knew that their journey was far from over.

"We're almost there," Thorne said, his voice breaking the silence. He pointed to a clearing up ahead, where the trees parted to reveal a grove bathed in a golden light.

As they stepped into the clearing, Seraphina felt a sense of peace and protection wash over her. The Sacred Grove was a place of immense power, its magic palpable in the air. At the center of the grove stood a massive, ancient oak tree, its branches reaching skyward like a cathedral.

"This place is incredible," Seraphina said, her voice filled with awe. "I can feel the magic here."

Thorne nodded, his eyes scanning the grove. "It's one of the most powerful places in the magical world. The grove has been a sanctuary for witches and magical beings for centuries."

As they approached the ancient oak, a figure emerged from the shadows. An old witch, her hair a cascade of silver and her eyes filled with wisdom, stood before them. She wore robes of deep green, adorned with symbols of protection and healing.

"Welcome to the Sacred Grove," the witch said, her voice resonant with age and power. "I am Isolde, guardian of this sacred place."

Seraphina and Thorne bowed respectfully. "Thank you for allowing us to seek refuge here," Seraphina said. "We have come seeking guidance and protection."

Isolde's eyes sparkled with understanding. "I know who you are and the trials you have faced. The grove has whispered your names to me. Come, let us sit by the ancient oak, and I will share with you what you need to know."

They followed Isolde to the base of the oak, where a circle of smooth stones formed a natural seating area. As they sat, Isolde began to speak, her voice weaving a tapestry of history and wisdom.

"The Sacred Grove has existed since the dawn of time, a place of refuge and healing for those who seek it. The magic here is ancient and powerful, bound to the very essence of the earth. It is said that the grove was created by the first witches, who sought a sanctuary from the darkness that plagued the world."

Seraphina and Thorne listened intently, their hearts filled with reverence for the ancient place and its guardian.

Isolde continued, "Your journey has been long and arduous, and you have faced many challenges. But there is one final step you must take to break the curse that binds you, Thorne."

Thorne's eyes met Isolde's, filled with hope and determination. "What must I do?"

Isolde's gaze was steady and compassionate. "The curse that binds you is tied to the very fabric of your soul. To break it, you must undergo the Rite of Soul Cleansing, a ritual that will purify your spirit and sever the ties that bind you to the curse. But be warned, the ritual is dangerous and requires immense strength and courage."

Seraphina's heart clenched with a mixture of fear and determination. "What does the ritual involve?"

Isolde's eyes softened. "The Rite of Soul Cleansing requires you to confront the darkest parts of your soul, the shadows that have plagued you for centuries. You must face your fears and your pain, and emerge stronger and purer. The ritual will take place here, in the Sacred Grove, where the magic is strongest. I will guide you, but the journey is yours alone to make."

Thorne nodded, his resolve unwavering. "I am ready. I will do whatever it takes to break this curse."

Seraphina's eyes filled with determination. "We will face this together, Thorne. Our bond is our greatest strength, and we will overcome this challenge."

Isolde's smile was gentle and wise. "Your love and commitment to each other are indeed powerful. Together, you can achieve what others might deem impossible. Rest tonight, and we will begin the ritual at dawn."

As the night fell over the Sacred Grove, Seraphina and Thorne prepared themselves for the ritual. They sat by the fire, the flames casting flickering shadows on their faces.

"Thorne," Seraphina said softly, her voice filled with emotion, "no matter what happens, I want you to know that I love you. You are not alone in this."

Thorne's eyes met hers, filled with gratitude and love. "I love you too, Seraphina. Your strength and support mean everything to me. Together, we can face anything."

As the fire burned low, they fell into a peaceful sleep, their dreams filled with images of the journey that lay ahead.

The dawn broke with a soft, golden light, and the Sacred Grove seemed to come alive with the promise of a new day. Isolde led Seraphina and Thorne to the base of the ancient oak, where the ritual would take place.

The air was thick with magic, and the grove was filled with the sounds of birds and rustling leaves. Isolde began to chant, her voice resonating with the ancient power of the grove.

"By the light of the dawn and the magic of the earth, we call upon the spirits of the Sacred Grove to guide us. We seek to purify the soul of Thorne Blackthorne and break the curse that binds him."

As Isolde chanted, a circle of light formed around Thorne, its energy pulsing with power. Seraphina stood just outside the circle, her heart pounding with anticipation and fear.

"Thorne," Isolde said, her voice filled with authority, "step into the circle and prepare to face the shadows of your soul."

Thorne took a deep breath and stepped into the circle, the light enveloping him in a cocoon of magic. He felt a surge of energy coursing through him, and his mind was filled with images of his past, the pain and the fear that had haunted him for centuries.

"Focus on the light," Isolde instructed. "Let it guide you as you confront the shadows within you."

Thorne closed his eyes and focused on the light, letting its warmth and power fill him. As he did, he felt the shadows of his past rising to the surface, the memories of betrayal and pain that had shaped his existence.

He saw the face of Alaric, the sorcerer who had cursed him, filled with malice and envy. He saw the faces of those he had lost, his family and friends, their expressions filled with sorrow and despair. He felt the weight of the centuries, the isolation and the longing for redemption.

But as the shadows surrounded him, Thorne felt the light growing stronger, its energy pushing back against the darkness. He focused on the love and support of Seraphina, her presence a beacon of hope and strength.

"Thorne," Seraphina's voice echoed in his mind, "you are not alone. We are in this together."

With a surge of determination, Thorne faced the shadows head-on, his resolve unbreakable. He confronted the pain and the fear, the guilt and the sorrow, and let the light of the Sacred Grove purify his soul.

The shadows began to dissipate, their grip on him weakening as the light grew stronger. Thorne felt a sense of peace and clarity washing over him, the weight of the curse lifting from his soul.

As the ritual reached its climax, Thorne felt a final surge of energy, the light enveloping him completely. The shadows were banished, and the curse was broken.

The light faded, and Thorne stood in the circle, his soul cleansed and his spirit free. He felt a sense of lightness and peace that he had not known for centuries.

Seraphina rushed to his side, her eyes filled with tears of joy and relief. "Thorne, you did it. The curse is broken."

Thorne's eyes met hers, filled with gratitude and love. "I couldn't have done it without you, Seraphina. Your strength and support were my guiding light."

Isolde's smile was gentle and proud. "You have faced the darkest parts of your soul and emerged stronger. The curse is broken, and you are free."

The grove seemed to hum with approval, the magic of the ancient place resonating with the triumph of the moment. Seraphina and Thorne embraced, their bond stronger than ever.

"Thank you, Isolde," Seraphina said, her voice filled with gratitude. "Your guidance has been invaluable."

Isolde nodded, her eyes filled with wisdom. "Your journey is far from over, but you have taken a significant step towards fulfilling your destiny. The Sacred Grove will always be a sanctuary for you, a place of healing and guidance."

As the day turned to night, Seraphina and Thorne sat by the fire, reflecting on the events of the day. The weight of the curse had been lifted, and they felt a sense of peace and hope that had been elusive for so long.

"Thorne," Seraphina said softly, her voice filled with love, "we have come so far, and I know that we can face whatever challenges come our way. Our bond is our greatest strength, and it will guide us through."

Thorne's eyes met hers, filled with gratitude and hope. "I believe in us, Seraphina. Together, we can overcome anything."

As they looked toward the future, their hearts filled with hope and determination, they knew that their journey was far from over. The Sacred Grove had given them the strength and guidance they needed to face the challenges ahead, and with each other by their side, there was nothing they could not achieve.

Their bond was unbreakable, their determination unwavering, and their love for each other and their bloodlines a powerful force that would guide them through the darkest of times. The Sacred Grove had revealed the depth of their strength and commitment, and with each other by their side, there was nothing they could not achieve.

In the days that followed, Seraphina and Thorne continued to learn and grow, their bond deepening with each passing moment. The Sacred Grove became a place of refuge and healing, a sanctuary where they could gather their strength and prepare for the trials ahead.

Isolde's wisdom and guidance were invaluable, and they learned much from her about the ancient magic of the grove and the history of their bloodlines.

The grove's magic seemed to resonate with their own, enhancing their abilities and deepening their connection.

One evening, as they sat by the fire with Isolde, she shared a final piece of wisdom. "The journey ahead will not be easy, but you have the strength and the bond to face it. Trust in each other and in the magic that flows through your veins. The Sacred Grove will always be with you, a source of strength and guidance."

Seraphina and Thorne nodded, their hearts filled with gratitude and determination. "Thank you, Isolde," Seraphina said. "We will carry your wisdom with us."

As they looked toward the horizon, their hearts filled with hope and determination, they knew that their journey was just beginning. The challenges they had faced had tested their commitment and bravery, but they had emerged stronger and more united than ever.

Their bond was unbreakable, their determination unwavering, and their love for each other and their bloodlines a powerful force that would guide them through the darkest of times. The Sacred Grove had revealed the depth of their strength and commitment, and with each other by their side, there was nothing they could not achieve.

As they set off on their next journey, the light of the Sacred Grove shining in their hearts, they knew that they were ready to face whatever lay ahead. Together, they would fulfill their destiny and protect the magical world from the forces of darkness. Their love and their bond would guide them through, and with each other by their side, there was nothing they could not achieve.

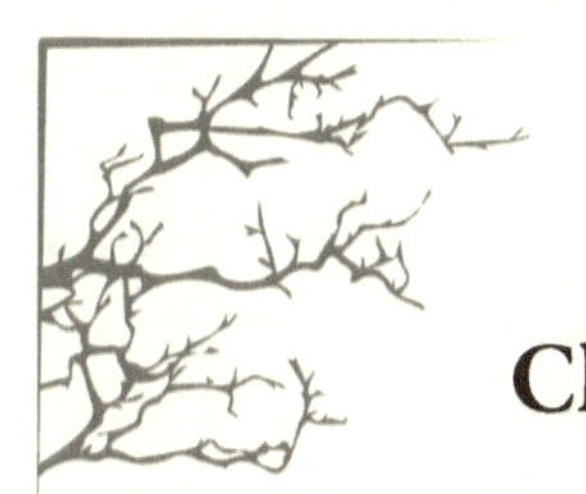

Chapter 13: The Final Confrontation

The tranquility of the Sacred Grove was a stark contrast to the dark storm brewing beyond its protective boundaries. Seraphina and Thorne had found refuge and strength in the ancient magic, but the threat of dark forces loomed ever closer. Their journey had been long and arduous, filled with trials that tested their bond and determination. Now, as they prepared for the final confrontation, the weight of the prophecy hung heavy on their hearts.

The sky darkened ominously, thick clouds rolling in to shroud the grove in an eerie twilight. Seraphina and Thorne stood at the center of the grove, the ancient oak tree looming protectively over them. Isolde, the wise guardian of the Sacred Grove, stood with them, her presence a beacon of calm and strength.

"The time has come," Isolde said, her voice steady and resonant. "The dark forces are converging upon us. You must be prepared for what lies ahead."

Seraphina nodded, her resolve unwavering. "We will face them together. Our bond is our greatest strength."

Thorne's eyes met hers, filled with determination and love. "No matter what happens, we will protect each other and fulfill the prophecy."

Isolde placed a hand on each of their shoulders, her gaze filled with a mixture of pride and sadness. "You have both shown immense courage and strength. Trust in the magic of the Sacred Grove and in your bond. The light will guide you."

As the first wave of dark energy crashed against the protective boundaries of the grove, the ground trembled and the air crackled with tension. The dark forces, led by the phantom hunter Lucien, had arrived.

Lucien stood at the edge of the grove, his eyes cold and unyielding. The betrayal he had once experienced had driven him to this moment, his vendetta against phantoms consuming him entirely. Now, he led an army of dark creatures, each one more malevolent than the last.

"Seraphina! Thorne!" Lucien's voice rang out, filled with venom. "Your time is up. Surrender now, and perhaps I will show mercy."

Seraphina stepped forward, her voice strong and defiant. "We will not surrender, Lucien. We will protect the Sacred Grove and fulfill the prophecy."

Lucien's eyes narrowed, and with a flick of his wrist, he unleashed a wave of dark energy towards them. Seraphina and Thorne reacted instantly, their combined magic forming a barrier of light that deflected the attack.

"Then you will fall," Lucien snarled, his army surging forward.

The battle that ensued was nothing short of epic. The air was filled with the clash of magic, the sounds of spells and the roars of dark creatures reverberating through the grove. Seraphina and Thorne fought with unwavering determination, their bond guiding their every move.

Seraphina's magic was precise and powerful, each spell designed to protect and support Thorne. Her connection to the Sacred Grove enhanced her abilities, and the light of the grove's magic pulsed through her veins. Thorne, now free of his curse, fought with a newfound strength and clarity. His magic was fierce and formidable, each spell a testament to his power and resolve.

Together, they were a force to be reckoned with, their love and determination driving them forward. But the dark forces were relentless, their attacks growing more intense with each passing moment.

In the midst of the chaos, Lucien confronted Thorne, his eyes filled with a mixture of hatred and desperation. "You should have never been freed, phantom. You are a threat to us all."

Thorne's eyes blazed with determination. "I am not the monster you believe me to be, Lucien. But if you seek a fight, you will have one."

The clash between Thorne and Lucien was intense, their magic colliding in a brilliant display of power. Thorne's determination and the strength of his bond with Seraphina fueled his attacks, but Lucien's hatred and skill made him a formidable opponent.

As Thorne and Lucien battled, Seraphina faced off against the dark creatures, her magic a beacon of light amidst the darkness. She fought with everything she had, her love for Thorne and her commitment to the prophecy giving her strength.

Despite their efforts, the tide of the battle began to turn. The dark forces were overwhelming, and Seraphina and Thorne were being pushed to their limits. Seraphina's heart pounded with fear and determination. She knew that they needed something more, something powerful enough to turn the tide.

In a moment of clarity, Seraphina remembered the words of Isolde and the prophecy that had guided them. The final step to breaking the curse and fulfilling the prophecy required a sacrifice, an ultimate act of love and bravery.

With a heavy heart, Seraphina realized what she had to do. She turned to Thorne, her eyes filled with love and determination. "Thorne, I know what we need to do. The prophecy requires a sacrifice. I must be the one to make it."

Thorne's eyes widened with fear and desperation. "No, Seraphina. I can't lose you. There must be another way."

Seraphina's voice was steady and resolute. "This is the only way. Our bond is our greatest strength, and it will guide us through. Trust me, Thorne."

With a deep breath, Seraphina stepped forward, her heart pounding with a mixture of fear and determination. She began to chant an incantation, her voice resonating with the ancient magic of the Sacred Grove.

"By the light of the dawn and the magic of the earth, I call upon the spirits of the Sacred Grove. Guide me as I make this sacrifice, and let the prophecy be fulfilled."

As she chanted, a circle of light formed around her, its energy pulsing with power. Thorne's eyes filled with tears as he watched, his heart breaking with the realization of what she was about to do.

"Seraphina, please," Thorne's voice was filled with desperation. "There must be another way."

Seraphina's eyes met his, filled with love and determination. "Trust in our bond, Thorne. This is the only way."

With a final surge of energy, Seraphina completed the incantation, the light enveloping her in a cocoon of magic. The ground trembled, and the air crackled with energy as the prophecy began to unfold.

The light grew brighter and more intense, and the dark forces recoiled, their attacks faltering. Lucien's eyes widened with fear and desperation as he realized what was happening.

"No!" Lucien shouted, his voice filled with rage. "This cannot be!"

But it was too late. The power of the prophecy was unstoppable, and the light of the Sacred Grove pulsed with an overwhelming force. The dark creatures were banished, their forms dissolving into the air.

As the light reached its peak, Seraphina felt a surge of energy coursing through her, her love for Thorne and her commitment to the prophecy giving her strength. She knew that this was the ultimate act of love and bravery, the final step needed to break the curse.

With a final, powerful incantation, Seraphina unleashed the full force of the prophecy, the light enveloping the entire grove. The ground shook, and the air was filled with a brilliant, blinding light.

When the light finally faded, the grove was silent. The dark forces were gone, banished by the power of the prophecy. Thorne stood at the center of the grove, his heart pounding with fear and hope.

"Seraphina," Thorne's voice was filled with desperation. "Where are you?"

As the dust settled, Thorne saw Seraphina lying on the ground, her form surrounded by a soft, ethereal glow. He rushed to her side, his heart breaking with fear.

"Seraphina, please," Thorne's voice was choked with emotion. "Please, wake up."

Seraphina's eyes fluttered open, her voice weak but filled with love. "Thorne, the prophecy... it's fulfilled. The curse is broken."

Thorne's eyes filled with tears of relief and gratitude. "You did it, Seraphina. You saved us all."

Isolde approached, her eyes filled with a mixture of pride and sadness. "You have both shown immense courage and strength. The prophecy is fulfilled, and the curse is broken. Seraphina's sacrifice was the ultimate act of love and bravery."

Seraphina smiled weakly, her heart filled with peace. "Our bond is our greatest strength, and it has guided us through."

Thorne's eyes met hers, filled with love and gratitude. "I love you, Seraphina. Thank you for everything."

Seraphina's eyes sparkled with tears. "I love you too, Thorne. We have faced so much together, and we have always come through."

As they embraced, the grove seemed to hum with approval, the magic of the ancient place resonating with the triumph of the moment. The prophecy had been fulfilled, and the curse was broken. The dark forces had been banished, and peace had been restored to the magical world.

In the days that followed, Seraphina and Thorne continued to heal and recover from the battle. The Sacred Grove remained a place of refuge and healing, its magic a source of strength and guidance.

Isolde's wisdom and guidance were invaluable, and they learned much from her about the ancient magic of the grove and the history of their bloodlines. The grove's magic seemed to resonate with their own, enhancing their abilities and deepening their connection.

One evening, as they sat by the fire with Isolde, she shared a final piece of wisdom. "The journey ahead will not be easy, but you have the strength and the bond to face it. Trust in each other and in the magic that flows through your veins. The Sacred Grove will always be with you, a source of strength and guidance."

Seraphina and Thorne nodded, their hearts filled with gratitude and determination. "Thank you, Isolde," Seraphina said. "We will carry your wisdom with us."

As they looked toward the horizon, their hearts filled with hope and determination, they knew that their journey was just beginning. The challenges they had faced had tested their commitment and bravery, but they had emerged stronger and more united than ever.

Their bond was unbreakable, their determination unwavering, and their love for each other and their bloodlines a powerful force that would guide them through the darkest of times. The Sacred Grove had revealed the depth of their strength and commitment, and with each other by their side, there was nothing they could not achieve.

As they set off on their next journey, the light of the Sacred Grove shining in their hearts, they knew that they were ready to face whatever lay ahead. Together, they would fulfill their destiny and protect the magical world from the forces of darkness. Their love and their bond would guide them through, and with each other by their side, there was nothing they could not achieve.

The final confrontation had tested their resolve and commitment, but it had also shown them the true strength of their love and their unity. With the prophecy fulfilled and the curse broken, they were ready to face the future, their bond stronger than ever.

Chapter 14: The Phantom's Liberation

The battle was over. The Sacred Grove, with its ancient trees and protective magic, had stood strong against the dark forces. The air, once filled with the sounds of conflict, now hummed with a serene silence. The prophecy had been fulfilled, and the curse that had bound Thorne for centuries was finally broken.

As dawn broke over the Sacred Grove, the first rays of sunlight pierced through the canopy, casting a warm, golden light on the forest floor. Seraphina, exhausted but resolute, knelt by Thorne's side. He lay unconscious, his body slowly undergoing the transformation from phantom to mortal form. The ethereal glow that had surrounded him during the final confrontation was fading, replaced by the vibrant hue of life returning to his veins.

Isolde, the wise guardian of the Sacred Grove, approached with a serene smile. "The curse is broken, Seraphina. Thorne is regaining his mortal form. Your sacrifice and love have made this possible."

Seraphina's heart swelled with relief and gratitude. She had given everything to save Thorne, and now, as she watched his transformation, she knew it had all been worth it. The bond they shared had proven to be their greatest strength, guiding them through the darkest of times.

As Thorne's transformation continued, the aftermath of the battle became more apparent. The Sacred Grove, despite its resilience, bore the scars of the conflict. Fallen branches and scorched earth marked the places where dark magic had clashed with the grove's protective enchantments. Yet, even amidst the damage, there was a sense of renewal and hope.

Seraphina and Isolde began to tend to the wounded and repair the damage. The coven members, some bearing injuries from the battle, worked tirelessly to restore the grove's natural harmony. Their efforts were a testament to their resilience and determination to protect their sanctuary.

Throughout the day, Seraphina's thoughts were never far from Thorne. She checked on him frequently, each time finding him a little more changed, a little more mortal. His skin, once pallid and ghostly, now had a healthy flush. His breathing, once non-existent, was now steady and rhythmic.

As evening fell, Thorne finally stirred. His eyes fluttered open, and he looked around in confusion before his gaze settled on Seraphina. "Seraphina," he whispered, his voice weak but filled with emotion. "Is it really over?"

Seraphina's eyes filled with tears of joy and relief. "Yes, Thorne. The curse is broken. You're free."

Thorne reached out, and Seraphina took his hand, feeling the warmth and life in his touch. It was a moment she had dreamed of for so long, and now it was finally real. They embraced, their hearts beating in unison, their bond stronger than ever.

The following days were a time of healing and reflection for the coven. The battle had taken its toll, and there were losses to mourn and wounds to heal. Seraphina and Thorne, though overjoyed at their newfound freedom, were not untouched by the grief that permeated the grove.

Seraphina spent hours with those who had lost loved ones, offering comfort and support. The sense of community and shared sorrow brought the coven closer together, strengthening their resolve to protect each other and their sanctuary.

One evening, as the sun set and the grove was bathed in a soft, golden light, a memorial ceremony was held for those who had fallen. The coven gathered around the ancient oak, their faces illuminated by the flickering light of candles. High Priestess Elowen led the ceremony, her voice filled with reverence and sorrow.

"We gather here to honor the brave souls who gave their lives to protect our sanctuary," Elowen said, her voice steady despite the tears in her eyes. "Their sacrifice will never be forgotten, and their spirits will always be with us."

As the ceremony continued, Seraphina felt a deep sense of gratitude and responsibility. The battle had been a turning point, and the losses endured had only strengthened her commitment to protecting the magical world and those she loved.

As Thorne continued to recover and adapt to his mortal form, he and Seraphina spent more time together, rediscovering their bond in a new light.

The transformation had not only freed Thorne from his curse but had also deepened their connection, allowing them to explore a future they had once thought impossible.

One afternoon, they sat by the edge of a tranquil pond within the grove, the water reflecting the vibrant colors of the surrounding flora. Thorne leaned against a tree, his eyes closed as he listened to the soothing sounds of nature.

"This place is incredible," Thorne said, his voice filled with wonder. "I can feel the life and magic all around us."

Seraphina smiled, her heart full. "The Sacred Grove has always been a sanctuary, a place of healing and renewal. It's where we found our strength and where we broke the curse."

Thorne opened his eyes and looked at her, his gaze filled with love and gratitude. "And it's where we can begin our new life together."

Seraphina's eyes sparkled with tears of joy. "I never dared to dream that this day would come, but now that it has, I can't imagine a future without you."

Thorne took her hand, his touch warm and reassuring. "We have faced so much together, and we have always come through. Our bond is our greatest strength, and it will guide us through whatever challenges lie ahead."

As they sat together, watching the sunset over the grove, they felt a sense of peace and hope that they had longed for. The future was filled with possibilities, and they were ready to face it together.

In the days that followed, Seraphina and Thorne began to plan for the future. The Sacred Grove, with its powerful magic and protective enchantments, would remain their sanctuary, but they also felt a calling to explore the wider world and fulfill their destiny.

High Priestess Elowen, ever wise and supportive, offered her guidance and blessings. "The prophecy has been fulfilled, but your journey is far from over. The magical world needs your strength and your bond. Trust in each other and in the magic that flows through your veins."

Seraphina and Thorne nodded, their hearts filled with determination. "We will carry your wisdom with us, High Priestess," Seraphina said. "And we will continue to protect the magical world and those we love."

As they prepared to leave the Sacred Grove and embark on their next journey, they felt a deep sense of gratitude for the sanctuary that had given them strength and the community that had supported them.

On the morning of their departure, the coven gathered to bid them farewell. The air was filled with a mixture of excitement and sorrow, the sense of an ending and a new beginning.

Isolde, the guardian of the Sacred Grove, approached Seraphina and Thorne, her eyes filled with pride and love. "You have both shown immense courage and strength. The Sacred Grove will always be with you, a source of strength and guidance."

Seraphina embraced Isolde, her heart filled with gratitude. "Thank you, Isolde. Your wisdom and guidance have been invaluable."

Thorne nodded, his eyes reflecting the same gratitude. "We will never forget what you have done for us."

As they left the grove, hand in hand, Seraphina and Thorne felt a sense of hope and determination that guided their steps. The journey ahead was filled with challenges and uncertainties, but they were ready to face them together.

Their travels took them through enchanted forests and mystical landscapes, each place filled with its own magic and wonders. They encountered other magical beings, some seeking help and others offering wisdom and guidance. The bond they shared and the experiences they had in the Sacred Grove had prepared them well, and they faced each challenge with unwavering determination.

One evening, as they camped by the edge of a crystal-clear lake, Thorne turned to Seraphina, his eyes filled with love and gratitude. "Seraphina, our journey has been long and filled with trials, but it has also brought us closer together. I can't imagine a future without you by my side."

Seraphina's eyes sparkled with tears of joy. "I feel the same, Thorne. Our bond is our greatest strength, and it will guide us through whatever lies ahead."

As they sat by the fire, the stars reflecting in the water, they felt a deep sense of peace and hope. The future was filled with possibilities, and they were ready to face it together.

Their journey eventually led them to a hidden valley, a place of unparalleled beauty and magic. The valley was home to an ancient temple, its walls adorned with intricate carvings and symbols of protection and healing. It was said that the temple held the wisdom of the ancients, a place where seekers could find answers to the deepest mysteries of the magical world.

As they approached the temple, Seraphina and Thorne felt a sense of reverence and awe. The air was thick with magic, and the sounds of nature seemed to harmonize with the energy of the place.

"Thorne, this place is incredible," Seraphina said, her voice filled with wonder. "I can feel the wisdom and magic all around us."

Thorne nodded, his eyes scanning the temple's intricate carvings. "It's like the Sacred Grove, but even more ancient and powerful. I think we can learn much here."

They entered the temple, their footsteps echoing in the vast, dimly lit hall. The walls were lined with scrolls and books, each one containing the knowledge and wisdom of the ancients. At the center of the hall stood a large, ornate altar, its surface covered with symbols of protection and healing.

As they approached the altar, a figure emerged from the shadows. An old wizard, his eyes filled with wisdom and kindness, stood before them. "Welcome, seekers," he said, his voice resonant and soothing. "I am Aldric, guardian of this ancient temple. What brings you to this sacred place?"

Seraphina and Thorne exchanged glances before Seraphina spoke. "We have come seeking wisdom and guidance. We have faced many trials and fulfilled a prophecy, but we know our journey is far from over."

Aldric nodded, his eyes filled with understanding. "You have indeed come to the right place. The temple holds the wisdom of the ancients, and it will guide you on your path. But first, you must prove your worthiness."

Thorne stepped forward, his voice steady and determined. "We are ready to face any challenge. Our bond is our greatest strength, and it has guided us through the darkest of times."

Aldric's smile was gentle and approving. "Very well. The first trial is one of knowledge. You must decipher the ancient symbols on the altar and unlock the wisdom contained within."

Seraphina and Thorne approached the altar, their minds focused and their hearts filled with determination. The symbols were intricate and complex, each one containing layers of meaning and power.

As they worked together, their bond guided their efforts, their combined knowledge and intuition allowing them to decipher the symbols. The air around them seemed to shimmer with magic, and the altar began to glow with a soft, golden light.

"Well done," Aldric said, his voice filled with approval. "You have proven your knowledge and understanding. The second trial is one of courage. You must face your deepest fears and emerge stronger."

Thorne's eyes met Seraphina's, filled with determination. "We have faced many fears together, and we will face this one as well."

Aldric led them to a chamber deep within the temple, its walls lined with mirrors. "This chamber will reveal your deepest fears. You must confront them and overcome them."

As they entered the chamber, the mirrors began to shimmer, their surfaces reflecting scenes of their past and the fears that had haunted them. Seraphina saw images of betrayal and loss, while Thorne saw the faces of those he had lost and the pain of his cursed existence.

But as they faced their fears, they felt the strength of their bond guiding them. They confronted the pain and the sorrow, the guilt and the fear, and emerged stronger and more united.

"You have shown great courage," Aldric said as they left the chamber. "The final trial is one of heart. You must demonstrate the depth of your love and commitment to each other."

Seraphina and Thorne stood before Aldric, their hearts filled with love and determination. "Our bond is unbreakable," Seraphina said, her voice steady. "We have faced so much together, and our love has guided us through."

Thorne nodded, his eyes filled with gratitude. "We are ready to face this trial together."

Aldric's smile was warm and approving. "Very well. You must each take a vow, a promise that will bind your hearts and souls together for eternity."

Seraphina and Thorne exchanged glances before taking each other's hands. "I vow to stand by your side, to love and protect you, and to face whatever challenges lie ahead with you," Seraphina said, her voice filled with emotion.

Thorne's eyes met hers, filled with love and determination. "I vow to be your strength and support, to love and protect you, and to face whatever challenges lie ahead with you."

As they made their vows, the air around them shimmered with magic, and a soft, golden light enveloped them. The temple seemed to hum with approval, and Aldric's eyes sparkled with pride.

"Your love and commitment are truly powerful," Aldric said. "You have passed the trials, and the wisdom of the ancients is now yours."

In the days that followed, Seraphina and Thorne immersed themselves in the knowledge and wisdom contained within the temple. They learned about the ancient magic that had shaped the world and the history of their bloodlines. The bond they shared and the experiences they had faced had prepared them well, and they felt a deep sense of purpose and determination.

One evening, as they sat by the fire in the temple's great hall, Thorne turned to Seraphina, his eyes filled with love and gratitude. "Seraphina, our journey has been long and filled with trials, but it has also brought us closer together. I can't imagine a future without you by my side."

Seraphina's eyes sparkled with tears of joy. "I feel the same, Thorne. Our bond is our greatest strength, and it will guide us through whatever lies ahead."

As they sat together, watching the fire dance and flicker, they felt a deep sense of peace and hope. The future was filled with possibilities, and they were ready to face it together.

Their journey eventually led them back to the Sacred Grove, their hearts filled with a sense of fulfillment and purpose. The grove, with its ancient trees and protective magic, welcomed them back with open arms.

Isolde, the wise guardian of the Sacred Grove, greeted them with a warm smile. "Welcome back, seekers. The grove has missed you."

Seraphina and Thorne embraced Isolde, their hearts filled with gratitude. "Thank you, Isolde. We have learned much and faced many trials, but we are stronger and more united than ever."

Isolde nodded, her eyes filled with pride and love. "The Sacred Grove will always be your sanctuary, a place of healing and guidance. Trust in each other and in the magic that flows through your veins."

As they looked toward the horizon, their hearts filled with hope and determination, they knew that their journey was just beginning. The challenges they had faced had tested their commitment and bravery, but they had emerged stronger and more united than ever.

Their bond was unbreakable, their determination unwavering, and their love for each other and their bloodlines a powerful force that would guide them through the darkest of times. The Sacred Grove had revealed the depth of their strength and commitment, and with each other by their side, there was nothing they could not achieve.

As they set off on their next journey, the light of the Sacred Grove shining in their hearts, they knew that they were ready to face whatever lay ahead. Together, they would fulfill their destiny and protect the magical world from the forces of darkness. Their love and their bond would guide them through, and with each other by their side, there was nothing they could not achieve.

The liberation of Thorne from his curse had been a turning point, and now, as they looked toward the future, they knew that their journey was far from over. But with their bond and their love, they were ready to face whatever challenges lay ahead. Together, they would continue to protect the magical world and fulfill their destiny, their hearts filled with hope and determination.

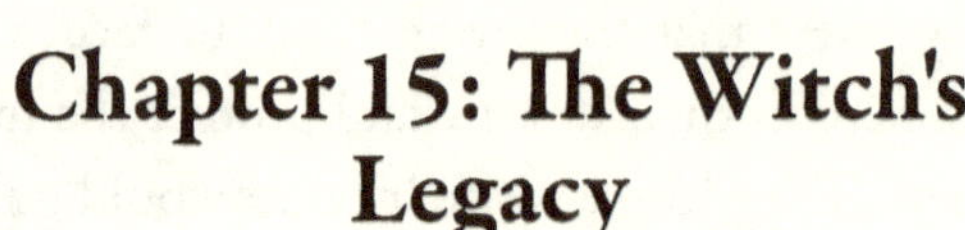

Chapter 15: The Witch's Legacy

The battle scars that marred the Sacred Grove were slowly healing, much like the wounds within the hearts of its inhabitants. The ancient trees, once twisted and torn by dark magic, stood tall and proud again, their leaves shimmering with renewed vitality. The grove had seen countless battles and witnessed immense sorrow, but it had also been a place of refuge, healing, and rebirth.

The prophecy had been fulfilled, and with Thorne's curse broken, the magical world could finally breathe a sigh of relief. However, with great power and responsibility bestowed upon them, Seraphina and Thorne knew that their journey was far from over. The coven needed a strong leader to guide them into this new era of peace and prosperity.

The morning sun cast a golden hue over the Sacred Grove as the coven members gathered around the ancient oak tree. High Priestess Elowen stood at the center, her wise eyes scanning the faces of those who had come to witness this pivotal moment. Seraphina and Thorne stood beside her, their hands clasped together, their bond and determination evident to all.

"Today, we stand at the dawn of a new era," Elowen began, her voice resonant with authority and reverence. "The prophecy has been fulfilled, and the dark forces that threatened our world have been vanquished. But with this victory comes the responsibility to rebuild and strengthen our coven, to ensure that the peace we have fought so hard for endures."

She turned to Seraphina, her gaze filled with pride and love. "Seraphina, you have shown immense courage, wisdom, and strength. You have led us through the darkest of times and emerged victorious. It is with great honor that I pass the mantle of leadership to you. May you guide us with the same dedication and love that you have shown throughout your journey."

Seraphina's heart swelled with emotion as she stepped forward, accepting the ceremonial staff that symbolized her new role as leader of the coven. "Thank you, High Priestess Elowen. I am humbled and honored by this responsibility. I promise to lead our coven with compassion, strength, and wisdom, and to protect the peace we have fought so hard to achieve."

The coven members erupted in applause and cheers, their faces alight with hope and admiration. Thorne squeezed Seraphina's hand, his eyes filled with love and pride. "You will be an incredible leader, Seraphina. I have no doubt."

The transition of leadership was seamless, thanks to Elowen's guidance and the unwavering support of the coven members. Seraphina quickly immersed herself in her new role, working tirelessly to rebuild and strengthen the coven. She sought to create an environment of unity, trust, and mutual respect, where every member felt valued and heard.

One of her first acts as leader was to establish a council of elders, composed of the most experienced and wise members of the coven. This council would provide guidance and support, ensuring that the coven's decisions were made with careful consideration and the collective good in mind.

"We have faced many challenges together," Seraphina addressed the council during their first meeting. "And we have emerged stronger because of it. Our bond is our greatest strength, and it is through unity and collaboration that we will continue to thrive."

The council members nodded in agreement, their faces reflecting the trust and respect they had for Seraphina. They knew that under her leadership, the coven would flourish.

As the days turned into weeks, Seraphina's vision for the coven began to take shape. She emphasized the importance of education and training, ensuring that every member had the opportunity to develop their magical abilities and knowledge. She organized regular workshops and seminars, inviting skilled practitioners from various magical disciplines to share their expertise.

Thorne, now fully embraced by the coven, played a pivotal role in these efforts. His extensive knowledge of ancient magic and his unique experiences as a former phantom made him an invaluable resource. He led training sessions on defensive magic, helping the coven members strengthen their protective enchantments and warding techniques.

One afternoon, during a particularly intense training session, Thorne demonstrated a powerful protective spell, his magic weaving a shimmering barrier that encircled the participants. "This barrier is designed to repel dark magic and protect against malevolent forces," he explained. "It draws on the energy of the earth and the strength of our bond. Remember, the key to powerful magic lies in your intent and your connection to the source of your power."

The coven members listened intently, their eyes filled with admiration and determination. They practiced the spell under Thorne's guidance, their confidence growing with each successful attempt.

Seraphina watched from the sidelines, her heart swelling with pride. Thorne had found his place within the coven, and together, they were creating a legacy of strength and unity.

The fulfillment of the prophecy brought peace not only to the Sacred Grove but to the entire magical world. News of their victory spread far and wide, and magical beings from all corners of the realm sought Seraphina's guidance and wisdom. The Sacred Grove became a beacon of hope and a sanctuary for those in need.

One evening, as Seraphina and Thorne sat by the edge of the tranquil pond, they reflected on the journey that had brought them to this moment. The water's surface mirrored the vibrant colors of the sunset, casting a warm glow over their faces.

"Thorne," Seraphina said softly, her voice filled with emotion. "We have come so far, and we have faced so much. I couldn't have done any of this without you."

Thorne's eyes met hers, filled with love and gratitude. "And I couldn't have done it without you, Seraphina. You are my strength, my guiding light. Together, we can face anything."

They sat in comfortable silence, their hearts beating in unison, their bond stronger than ever. The future was filled with possibilities, and they were ready to embrace it together.

Under Seraphina's leadership, the coven flourished. The Sacred Grove, once a place of refuge and healing, now thrived as a center of knowledge, unity, and strength. The bonds between the coven members grew stronger, their collective magic a force to be reckoned with.

Seraphina's emphasis on education and training paid off, as the coven members became more skilled and confident in their abilities. They developed new spells and enchantments, drawing on the ancient magic of the grove and the wisdom of their ancestors. The council of elders provided invaluable guidance, ensuring that the coven's decisions were made with wisdom and foresight.

Thorne continued to play a vital role, leading training sessions and sharing his knowledge of ancient magic. His experiences as a former phantom gave him a unique perspective, and his insights were highly valued by the coven members. He and Seraphina worked closely together, their partnership a testament to the strength of their bond.

One evening, as they sat by the fire in the great hall, Seraphina turned to Thorne, her eyes filled with love and gratitude. "Thorne, I am so grateful for your support and your love. Together, we have achieved so much, and I know that we can achieve even more."

Thorne took her hand, his touch warm and reassuring. "Seraphina, our bond is our greatest strength. With you by my side, I know that we can face anything and everything that comes our way."

As they looked toward the future, their hearts filled with hope and determination, they knew that their journey was far from over. The challenges they had faced had tested their commitment and bravery, but they had emerged stronger and more united than ever.

The fulfillment of the prophecy brought peace to the magical world, and the Sacred Grove became a symbol of hope and resilience. The coven's efforts to rebuild and strengthen their sanctuary were recognized and celebrated by magical beings from all corners of the realm. The grove's protective enchantments were reinforced, and its ancient magic continued to thrive.

One day, as Seraphina and Thorne walked through the grove, they were approached by a group of young witches and wizards. Their eyes were filled with admiration and excitement.

"Seraphina, Thorne," one of the young witches said, her voice filled with awe. "We have heard so much about your journey and the prophecy. We aspire to be like you, to protect our world and to create a legacy of strength and unity."

Seraphina's heart swelled with pride and warmth. "Thank you for your kind words. Remember that true strength comes from within and from the bonds we share with those we love. Trust in your abilities, and always strive to do what is right."

Thorne nodded, his eyes filled with encouragement. "You have the potential to achieve great things. Believe in yourselves and in the power of your magic. Together, we can create a better world."

The young witches and wizards nodded eagerly, their faces alight with determination. Seraphina and Thorne continued their walk, their hearts filled with hope for the future.

As the seasons changed, the coven continued to thrive under Seraphina's leadership. The Sacred Grove, with its ancient trees and protective magic, remained a sanctuary of peace and knowledge. The bonds between the coven members grew stronger, their collective magic a force of harmony and protection.

Seraphina and Thorne's partnership was a beacon of love and unity. They faced each challenge together, their bond guiding them through the uncertainties of the magical world. Their love was a testament to the strength and resilience that had carried them through the darkest of times.

One evening, as they sat by the fire in their cozy cottage within the grove, Seraphina turned to Thorne, her eyes filled with love and contentment. "Thorne, our journey has been long and filled with trials, but it has also brought us closer together. I can't imagine a future without you by my side."

Thorne's eyes met hers, filled with gratitude and devotion. "I feel the same, Seraphina. Our bond is our greatest strength, and it will guide us through whatever lies ahead."

As they sat together, watching the fire dance and flicker, they felt a deep sense of peace and fulfillment. The future was filled with possibilities, and they were ready to embrace it together.

The prophecy's fulfillment had brought peace to the magical world, and Seraphina's leadership ensured that this peace endured. The coven's efforts to rebuild and strengthen their sanctuary were recognized and celebrated by magical beings from all corners of the realm. The Sacred Grove became a beacon of hope and resilience, a symbol of the strength and unity that had guided them through the darkest of times.

Seraphina and Thorne's legacy was one of love, strength, and unity. Their bond had been tested and proven unbreakable, their love a guiding light through the uncertainties of the magical world. Together, they had created a legacy that would endure for generations to come.

As they looked toward the horizon, their hearts filled with hope and determination, they knew that their journey was far from over. The challenges they had faced had tested their commitment and bravery, but they had emerged stronger and more united than ever.

Their bond was unbreakable, their determination unwavering, and their love for each other and their bloodlines a powerful force that would guide them through the darkest of times. The Sacred Grove had revealed the depth of their strength and commitment, and with each other by their side, there was nothing they could not achieve.

As they set off on their next journey, the light of the Sacred Grove shining in their hearts, they knew that they were ready to face whatever lay ahead. Together, they would fulfill their destiny and protect the magical world from the forces of darkness. Their love and their bond would guide them through, and with each other by their side, there was nothing they could not achieve.

The witch's legacy was one of hope, strength, and unity, and it would endure for generations to come. Seraphina and Thornc's journey was far from over, but they were ready to face it together, their hearts filled with love and determination. Together, they would continue to protect the magical world and fulfill their destiny, their bond and their love guiding them through the darkest of times.

Don't miss out!

Visit the website below and you can sign up to receive emails whenever Sarah Elizabeth Davis publishes a new book. There's no charge and no obligation.

https://books2read.com/r/B-A-METXB-MVWIE

BOOKS2READ

Connecting independent readers to independent writers.

Did you love *The Witch's Phantom*? Then you should read *The Phantom's Revenge*[1] by Sarah Elizabeth Davis!

Emily Hartman inherits an old mansion from her great-grandmother, only to find it haunted by a vengeful spirit known as "The Phantom." As Emily delves into the mansion's dark history, she uncovers a tragic tale of love and betrayal. With the help of local historian Jack, Emily must solve the mystery of the Phantom's curse before it claims her life. In a race against time, she faces supernatural encounters, unearths hidden secrets, and ultimately seeks justice to bring peace to the restless spirit. "The Phantom's Revenge" is a gripping tale of mystery, love, and redemption.

---

1. https://books2read.com/u/b6goNx

2. https://books2read.com/u/b6goNx

About the Author

Sarah Elizabeth Davis is a celebrated author in the fantasy collections and anthologies genre. Known for her captivating storytelling, she crafts intricate tales that transport readers to magical realms. Raised in a town rich with folklore, her passion for fantasy was kindled early on. With a degree in English Literature, Sarah has published acclaimed anthologies, earning a loyal following. When not writing, she enjoys exploring new places and spending time with family and pets. Sarah's work, filled with wonder and adventure, continues to enchant readers and leave a lasting impact on the literary world.